## Praise for *As Luck Would Have It*

'This is a strange novel, hard to forget, that ostensibly sets out to tell the story of an orphan's emergence into a frightening world of mysterious or eccentric adults. Covertly, however, the book is a fairytale about magical transformations and unexpected redemption. Every word (tentative, revised, timidly advanced) counts in this fable. The tone is so mesmerizing that the narrator, far from being a neutral observer, turns into the most original character...'   Edmund White

'*As Luck Would Have It*, which is set in the drab London of the 1950s, is an understated study of repression and reticence. If its characters seem to be living half-lives, that is because Samuel Lock knows and understands that in, pre-Wolfenden Report England, homosexual men and women had to be secretive. The narrative tone of this subtle novel is perfectly sustained, whilst the period is recreated without an excess of nudging details.'  Paul Bailey

'I've never read anything quite like it ... a genuinely surreal book ... governed by the impeccable prosiness of a vivid dream.' James Merrill

'With its strange, philosophical serenity, prose stylishness and fey plotting, it could be destined for cult status. It is clearly a one-off; it is also one-of-a-kind.'  Ian Sansom, *Sunday Telegraph*

'A delight ... a wonderful period piece. *As Luck Would Have It* is humorous, tender and original.'  Sebastian Beaumont, *Gay Times*

'Strange, affecting, offbeat ... its rather naive first-person narration has a freshness that is both unique and endearing.'  Christie Hickman, *Midweek*

D1332377

Samuel Lock was born in 1926. He has worked as a painter and stage designer, and as a scriptwriter in the documentary cinema. He is the author of five plays and this is his first novel.

# As Luck Would Have It

## SAMUEL LOCK

JONATHAN CAPE
LONDON

First published 1995

3 5 7 9 10 8 6 4

© Samuel Lock 1995

Samuel Lock has asserted his right under the Copyright, Designs and
Patents Act, 1988 to be identified as the author of this work

First published in the United Kingdom in 1995 by
Jonathan Cape
Random House, 20 Vauxhall Bridge Road, London SW1V 2SA

Random House Australia (Pty) Limited
20 Alfred Street, Milsons Point, Sydney,
New South Wales 2061, Australia

Random House New Zealand Limited
18 Poland Road, Glenfield,
Auckland 10, New Zealand

Random House South Africa (Pty) Limited
PO Box 337, Bergvlei, 2012 South Africa

Random House UK Limited Reg. No. 954009

A CIP catalogue record for this book
is available from the British Library

Papers used by Random House UK Limited are natural, recyclable products
made from wood grown in sustainable forests. The manufacturing processes
conform to the environmental regulations of the country of origin.

ISBN 0-224-04251-3

Typeset by Deltatype Ltd, Ellesmere Port, Cheshire
Printed and bound in Great Britain by
Mackays of Chatham PLC, Chatham, Kent

The way ascends not straight, but imitates
The subtle foldings of a winter's snake.

John Webster
*The White Devil*

# I

IF YOU HAVE a prejudice against men who are ambivalent;
or who like dressing up in women's clothes, and things like
that; then you'd better not read this book. Not that there'll
be much in it about the latter – about men in drag, I mean –
because I've never actually met any of those; or not up close,
that is; although I did once know a dentist living in Barnes, I
think it was, or Richmond, who used to insist, each time he
washed his hair, upon borrowing a hairnet from his wife;
and who, with its silken band tucked beneath his chin,
would moon about the place all day, looking like some art-
deco advertisement. And on a train once going to Reading, I
was sitting in one of those open-style compartments – or
carriages, rather – the seatbacks of which were extremely
low in those days, and I happened to see this upright,
middle-aged woman I felt sure must be a man.

I can recall how it was a hot, midsummer afternoon, with
not many people on the train; and I was reading, or had been
reading, a book or magazine or something, and wasn't quite
conscious of where I was, nor of who was sitting around me.
Then, as I looked up, I saw beyond me, in the next group of
seats, this woman with a thick, strong-looking neck. A neck
so thick, in fact, so strong-looking, I felt sure it couldn't be
female. Then, when I looked closer, I could see a faint blue
shadow beneath the cheek and on the chin.

Was it a man? I thought to myself. Could it be? The image
was so mysterious; and beautiful too, I thought – particularly
since no-one else in the carriage appeared to have noticed it.

The woman looked at me and caught my eye. I couldn't quite tell whether she had read my thoughts or not. Perhaps she had though, because she immediately extracted from her handbag one of those neat, enamel-backed powder compacts that women carried with them in those days; and using it, began to powder not just her nose but her chin as well. Then, when the train stopped, and as she rose from her seat to leave, I could see by the way she walked, and by the knotted hardness of her calves, that this was indeed no woman. Yet, as she picked her way along the station platform, dressed in her neat, navy-blue suit; and wearing, pushed slightly to one side, a neat, navy-blue hat; she seemed almost to dissolve into the crowd.

There was just one other occasion when I saw such a figure – a transvestite, that is, as I later learned that they were called – and that was in the Orchard Room at Selfridges, where there used to be this long green bar, where you could sit and order sandwiches and things; and there beside me, or almost beside me, perched upon a high green and chromium stool, was this old hag of a thing with loosely fitting teeth, wearing a strawberry-coloured turban. And it seemed to me, that her disguise was far less subtle than had been the man's I had seen on the train: yet, as she slopped away at her ice-cream sundae, no-one seemed to notice her, or to look at her with any question in their eye; and failed to see what I had found so obvious.

Putting that first aside aside, however, it was shortly after Christmas; and Chuck and I had just moved into a flat – in South Kensington, close to the station. It had been his idea, I must hasten to add. We had met only a few weeks earlier, in a hostel for young people new to London; and disliking the place so much had agreed to share – or, rather, I had agreed to share with him.

'I've found this flat,' he told me abruptly. 'It's shabby,

but there's two decent-sized rooms; so how about us sharing; about us getting the hell out of here; out of this shitty-arsed hole?'

That is what he said to me, in a down-to-earth, matter-of-fact sort of way. And with terrific force, which there always seemed to be in his voice, whenever he had made up his mind about something. For he spoke quietly then, or comparatively quietly; and not in the rather campy voice that he generally used.

From this I learned that he was a very tough customer indeed; and that one shouldn't be confused by this habit he had of speaking to everyone as being their Auntie Zee. 'Auntie Zee told you,' he would say to people, if he wanted to point out to them that he had been right about something and they had been wrong. Or, 'It's Auntie Zee here,' he would chortle into the telephone, whenever he rang someone up.

He was enormous. By that I mean not just six foot five or six, but also big in build; and quite bouncy with it; and always seeming to be cheerful. But I'd never cross him – over anything; for if I did, then I knew that some dark side of him might emerge, and that he then could be quite frightening.

The thing about Chuck, or Chuckles, as he sometimes called himself – although his real name was Bruce – was that, from every point of view, he had such a huge, such a tremendous physique. Not that I had seen him in the raw, as it were, at the time we took this flat together; for you mustn't think that we were lovers. In fact, we were both quite coy at first about the sight of our undressed bodies; not quite liking to be naked, or even half naked, when the other was around.

Today, I believe that young people are much less shy than they were then, in the nineteen-fifties. It's nothing now to be in the nude – particularly indoors. And that's a good thing, I'm sure. But young people are in any case much shyer than they like to admit – even today, I expect. They brag about having done this or that; and, if they are male, will sit around telling each other smutty stories and the like; about the curate who had an erection, and that kind of thing: but when it comes to actually *doing* something: something not collective, that is, that exposes them, then they fight shy of it. Or that is how it seems to me.

But not in private, perhaps. Not, that is, in their secret world; in their fantasy world. Then, perhaps, they have a wildness that has to come out, and that *does* come out; and shyness goes by the board. I know, for instance, when I was at technical college (I'd better not give its name) I was shocked to the core by what went on. Not openly, but at night; when all the lights were out. To begin with, there were secret initiation ceremonies that were quite horrendous, but which, because I despised them so much, I have blotted from my mind: and then there was this father-son thing between the older students and the younger ones. Not something noble and upright, as it might sound, but simply an excuse for getting rid of erotic fantasies; in which the younger students were obliged to play the part of girls. Which meant that in secret, as I say, when all the college lights had been extinguished, there would be this heavy petting going on all over the place. Hugs and kisses, and quick heavy breathing – particularly from the hefties in the rugby team. Yet, oddly enough, they (the rugby team, I mean) despised those few – and it was just a few – who did what they did openly, and formed themselves into a clique; sitting about combing their hair and things; or singing songs made famous then by Judy Garland.

To this small band, I myself did not belong; for I was in no way sure of my sexual identity; and never courted, as they did, the favours of one of the lecturers who was known to be

4

keen on boys, and allowed themselves to be invited to his rooms. Or who, on other occasions, would make brazenly open visits to an ex-American-army chaplain, who had stayed on here after the war; and who, as they had discovered, had a similar weakness for young men. But I cannot deny that, as I got used to it, I derived some kind of kick, if not deep pleasure, out of that heavy midnight snogging: and each night, lying upon my bed, with the door of my room half open, I would wonder who might come to me; and who, having stepped inside and turned the key, would take me in their arms and hold me tight.

I suppose that in a sense I have always been the son-figure in such a relationship; and I suppose I was that with Chuck: though in a way, as I can now see, he was perhaps more of a mum to me than a dad; and this, perhaps, was the reason why we eventually had to part.

One day, when we had been in the flat for a couple of weeks, and I had got used to this view we had of all those museums – The Victoria and Albert, The Science, The Natural History and so on – Chuck came in with a great suitcase full of something, which he stuffed into a cupboard.

'Not for Bobo,' he said, with a wag of one fat finger – Bobo was a name he had invented for me, to put me down, I rather think; and then, with a quick flick of his wrist, turned the key in the cupboard door, extracted it, pocketed it, laughed to himself and went out.

'Just to get some milkies,' he called out as he left. 'Naughty Bobo,' he could be heard crying on the stairs: 'Got no milkies in for breakfast.'

And it was true that I had not, and like him too, I must admit, not to punish me for my omission. For if, as I was to learn later, he was something of a sadist, it never expressed itself through petty things; and as in this case, he had such an excess of physical energy, that to run downstairs to the street and back cost him no extra effort at all; and was, I suppose, in a way, much easier for him, and much more satisfying, then asking me to make the trip.

So in no time he was back; bearing not only pints of milk, but also other various 'goodies', as he used to speak of them, that had caught his eye; such as a large French loaf.

'Chuckles is very, very hungry,' he said: then looked at me with a devilish twinkle in his eye; as though, perhaps, though he never did, he might like to taunt me – perhaps, even, I used to think, to torture me; as though, if he had given into it, he might have gained some curious kind of pleasure from stuffing himself with food in front of me, and watching me go hungry.

In so many ways – in fact, in almost every way, this flat of ours was a relief. To begin with, there were no women about the place; for in the hostel, which lodged only young men, the staff was entirely female. Older women mostly, who either cleaned the rooms or changed the beds, and who seemed to be perpetually spying on people on the stairs. And the place was run by one of those snooty old women who think they are God Almighty, and behave as if all men are beneath them – especially younger ones.

I remember how we had to pay our rent to her in cash – each Friday; and in person. And that in order to do this, we almost had to grovel: in the sense, I mean, that she made it so humiliating; forcing us to wait outside her door and things; and then, as we were handing her the money, having some snide remark up her sleeve; like saying something about your sheets being dirty, or suggesting there had been someone in your room – someone other than yourself; with you, I mean.

She used to give me the creeps. Tall, cold, grey, with her hair parted at the centre and drawn back into a bun. And she hated men, and all things male. I used to think, and indeed did know, that she was dangerous; and for that reason, dreaded those Friday evenings after work, when I would wait in line until my turn had come, and one of her nasty little assistants would usher me into her parlour.

Sometimes, I even had fantasies that she would pounce on me, and that out from behind the woodwork, so to speak, would spring a whole band of women; who would then set on me – and, having robbed me of all that I possessed, would do me in.

So I was naturally glad to get away from there, and to have this view, as I say, of those dreamy, Victorian palaces that stood for Art and Science and the like. Not that they stood for either in a very substantial way, I used to think. For all their size – and, I suppose, grandeur, they never quite seemed to be present. And even today, if I should happen to pass them on a bus, I get this feeling that they aren't quite there; and that they are in fact not really built of stone at all; but are mere projections: things springing to life out of some set of period watercolours.

John Ruskin (you will have heard of him) had this thing, didn't he, about architecture not being the building itself, but the decoration that is applied to it. And I sometimes think that this must be the cause of all my troubles. That may sound a crazy thing to say, but you know what I mean. There was something about the Victorians that was really phoney. They spoke with authority about things, and laid down the law, as if they knew everything; and yet, when you come to look into it, so much of what they said was false – untrue. I mean, fancy their thinking what they did about Lord Leighton; that he was a god, more or less, and an inheritor of Michelangelo and the like; and paying the earth, as they did, for those phoney paintings he used to paint. And all that's inside us. All that phoniness, I mean.

One day – or evening, rather, for it was almost dark,

Chuck came home early. He used to work as a teller in the City, in one of the big City banks; and usually came home at about six. But this once he was early; and he said to me as he came in, 'Bobo,' he said, 'Chuckles is going out. Going to have a night on the tiles'; and with that, unlocked that cupboard of his; where, as I told you earlier, he had chosen to store his suitcase.

'Now then,' he chortled. 'Bobo's going to see Chuckles in his gear ... Never seen Chuckles in his gear – have you, Bobo?' he went on, as he placed the suitcase upon his bed and opened it. 'Never seen his Auntie Zee in his gear, has Bobo' – and with that, he drew out, piece by piece, laying them upon the counterpane as he did so, a series of curious leather garments that quite astonished me.

I don't know why, but I had never thought of Chuck as being a 'leather man'. I suppose it was *his* brand of phoniness that kept it from me: that way he had of pretending that he was your aunt or something – or your mum; so that, by the use of this curious device, he could remain in hiding, so to speak; and even from one who lived as close to him as I did.

But Chuck didn't change his clothes in front of me – not even his shirt. Instead, he gathered that gear of his together and took it with him into the bathroom, where he remained for quite some time; and which provided me with the chance I had been needing to adjust myself; and to rebuild (as I now knew that I must) the mental picture that I had formed of him during the time of our brief acquaintanceship.

I suppose I must be a very reflective sort of person; and had I been educated in a more proper fashion, and been taught to channel that aspect of my nature, I could, perhaps, have been a real thinker. By that I mean that at moments such as this, when a pause would occur, and I would be waiting for someone, as I was now waiting for Chuck, I would immediately fall into a kind of trance. I wouldn't think about myself. I wouldn't go and wash a pair of socks, for instance, as I might have done on that occasion; or ring someone up; or think about what I intended doing with the evening – with *my* evening, that is. Instead, I would sort of – well, reflect: and usually thoughts of various kinds would begin to assemble themselves in my mind. Not particular ones, but general ones; and ones that were usually philosophical in character.

On this occasion, I can remember thinking how mysterious people are, and how all of us use some kind of illusion or deceit – some mask, as one might speak of it, behind which we are able to hide. And we do this in order to hide as much away from ourselves as away from others.

I could see, for example, that Chuck had very separate parts of his mind, and that, in a way, he was never one whole person. That he was constructed out of different strands and features of his personality, that functioned quite separately from each other. One being this sprucely dressed figure, who left each morning for the City; and who, as he travelled upon the tube, must have seemed like all the other 'gents' around him. Another being this rather curious, flouncy, auntie-like figure, that kept referring to itself as your Auntie Zee. And now, as I had just discovered, there was this other – this more hidden side of his being; which, until then, I had only noticed in his voice – and when, as I said, I would feel afraid of him. A dark side of his personality that he showed to hardly anyone; but which now, for some reason, and within the privacy of our apartment, he had decided to reveal to me.

I remember wondering whether this was quite an event for him – this sudden sharing of his secret; and for that reason became all the more curious about that moment for which I had been waiting, when Chuck would appear before me in his gear. I cannot say that I was in any way nervous about it. That is the thing about curiosity – it stifles fear, and even caution. The desire for knowledge, and through that understanding, can over-ride all the coarser emotions; and I had already learned that this was one of my strengths: that, although I was in certain ways as timid as a mouse, about life and about people in general, if I became curious about something – if, in short, it interested me – then my timidity would disappear; and I would stand fearless and calm before whatever might confront me; ready to embrace the shocks or the surprises that it might hold in store.

And I have learned, as I have grown older, that life is exceedingly various; and that there are indeed as many computations of the human psyche – as many varieties of its structure – as there are people: so that I have learned to take a delight in, rather than to be shocked by, the idiosyncracies of my fellow human beings; and have found that nothing is more moving, because it is so enlightening, than the sudden shifts gained in perspective through an awareness of such things.

Thus it was that as I waited for Chuck – who I had known until then only as a rather smart city gentleman or as my bouncy Auntie Zee – I could see that I was preparing myself for such a shift in my understanding; in much the same way as I had been affected in such a manner when a friend of mine who was an analyst (this was much later in my life) told me of the success he had achieved with a patient of his, who had been in trouble with the police.

Apparently he – the patient, I mean – had a fixation to do with donkeys; which could only release itself (I wasn't told how) through certain forms of erotic play: and because of this (and because, of course, it's not easy to meet up with a donkey these days) he would haunt the stables of certain seaside resorts, where donkeys were still being bred; and which, of course (with his having been caught there on occasions) had involved him with the law.

Yet the achievement my friend had spoken of, and of which he had been so proud, was not one of a cure, but simply one of a transference; and not on to humans, as one might think, but on to dogs. Which meant, of course, that what the patient had lived out publicly, in donkeys' stables, he was now at liberty to indulge in within the privacy of his home.

Musing in this fashion, the sound of the bathroom door being unbolted came as a shock; for it had not occurred to me that Chuck would lock himself in. Which meant that before I had time to gather myself together, and so be prepared for the event, I found myself confronting what I now picture to myself as being some peculiar apparition: for there, trembling before me (there is no other word that will describe the quaint vibrations that he emanated) was no Auntie Zee, no smart-suited city gentleman, but a towering, tottering figure dressed from head to toe in black: a black that was relieved here and there by gleaming silver studs. So that he appeared almost as some figure of the night: not as frightening or as menacing as I had imagined he might be, but curiously at home and at ease with himself; as though I was being shown some deeper aspect of his personality: an aspect of which I had been ignorant, until that day – that moment – when I had first been shown his suitcase; and when, just a short while ago, its contents had been revealed to me.

I cannot say whether Chuck was offended by my response to his regalia or not. Had he expected me to be shocked, I wondered, or frightened; and was he, in turn, being forced to confront an aspect of my *own* nature with which he, as yet, was unfamiliar? Whatever, I can recall how he stood there – literally trembling, as I say – and asked, with a degree of caution in his voice (and even, I must admit, a degree of shyness that was almost coy) whether I liked his guise or not.

'So what do you think of it?' he asked, in a surprisingly soft tone of voice. 'Do you like it, Bobo?'

I told him (which was something of a lie) that I found the effect of his gear quite startling; quickly realising that this was an important event for him, and that he was anxious that I should be impressed.

'Oh,' he added, his eyes turning inward. 'I'm pleased, Bobo – *very*. I wanted you to like it.'

'And I *do*, Chuck. I really do . . . I think it's great,' I said – if we used that word in those days; though I suspect it might have been something more like super or fantastic; 'I had no idea, Chuck. None.'

'I thought you hadn't,' Chuck answered with a smile, and in a voice that had now grown even softer than before. 'Do you want anything, Bobo – before I go out? Do you want me to fetch you something; from the grocer's, I mean?'

The thought of Chuck descending to the street in all that leather, and of his then entering our local grocery store, appalled me; for we were both quite well known there by this time; and I could hardly think that it would improve our image to have Chuck walk in like that. One never knows, of course. As I said earlier, people are very various; and it could have been that the man who ran the grocery store would have expressed no astonishment whatsoever at the sight of Chuckles in his gear; or, even if he *had* been taken by surprise, might have thought little or nothing of it.

However, I decided to be careful, and so be my usual timid self; and quickly told Chuck that there was nothing at all that I needed, and that my plan was to read for a while and then go out: to our local pub, perhaps – where, I added (simply because that thought came into my head) I might possibly bump into George.

A nasty silence followed this remark, and I knew at once that, after our first two weeks in the flat together, I had touched upon ground that was somewhat dangerous; and that, although, as I have already said to you, we were in no way an affair; and that we were even shy as yet of sharing the sight of our naked bodies; Chuck felt for me – or, at least, had come to feel for me – something that I in no way felt for him.

'You're not seeing *him*, are you?' he growled at me, as if in pain. 'Not seeing that big, Northern thing – are you? Don't tell me you are, Bobo – *please*.' (The please was said with a curious slur.)

'Well, not on purpose, Chuck,' I answered quickly. 'I just thought that he *might* be there – that's all. He goes there regularly.'

'Regularly?'

'Yes.'

'George does?'

'Yes.'

'To our pub?'

'Yes.'

'The one around the corner?'

'Yes. You know he does. You know he goes there.'

'Oh.' Chuck's eyes avoided my own for a moment. 'I'd forgotten,' he said in a vague sort of way. 'So you mean – ?'

'He might *be* there. Yes. I might bump into him.'

With that, the danger appeared to pass; and there then entered into that companion of mine some kind of force, or some kind of energy, that quite took me by surprise. For with a sharp stamp of his heavily booted foot, as if he might be announcing the raising of some curtain at a theatre, he swung swiftly into action.

'I'm off then,' he muttered darkly. 'See you later . . . If someone calls – Darby or someone, say I'm out. Say I'm off on my bike' – and with that, he collected from that cupboard of his, where previously his suitcase had been stored, a dome-like silver helmet, which he then placed upon his head; and which, I have to confess, transformed him absolutely.

George was not at the pub, and I felt relieved. Chuck had steamed away on his motorbike, which I later learned he had borrowed from a friend; and I had watched him from our window as he had turned out of the small alleyway below, and had screeched off down the Brompton Road, his helmet all aglow with golden light: a light that it had attracted from the streetlights overhead, their colour heightened by the threat of sulphureous fog.

And if George *had* been there at the pub? What would I have actually said to Chuck, I found myself wondering. Would I have told him, or said nothing? Or would I have said, perhaps, that he *hadn't* been there; and by so doing lied? Certainly, I thought later in the evening, things between Chuck and myself had changed. For the first time since I had known him (which, as I told you, was no more than a matter of weeks) I had understood, in that moment of revelation, when he had appeared before me in his gear, that he had formed some kind of projection upon my person: that within the time of our brief acquaintanceship, there had developed within that mind of his some kind of possessive form of affection, which, if I weren't careful, could provoke him to be jealous.

Yet jealous of what, I asked myself – of George? Quite frankly, such an idea seemed preposterous: so much so, in fact, that it made me want to laugh. For I knew George much less well than I knew Chuck, having met him even more recently; and also at the hostel; and during the last few days of our stay there.

He – George, I mean – was a Scot. An engineer – or one to be, rather. He was calm, steady, tall, well-built (though not as tall as Chuck) and quite striking in his looks: blond, with a near-white, blemish-free skin that was curiously opaque: so that, at times, one could almost think that he wore make-up. He didn't smoke, as Chuck and I did, and his use of the pub – or of 'our' pub, as Chuck referred to it – was due to it being the pub we had gone to from the hostel, it lying roughly halfway between that establishment and our new abode.

I certainly liked him – meaning George; enjoying his reasonableness, his cleanliness, the flat even tones of his voice. And when I had said to Chuck that I might perhaps bump into him, I suppose there could have been, at the very back of my mind, some kind of hope that he would be there.

But it was only the very faintest of desires. Nothing in me, in those days, seemed much stronger than that. Indeed, I must have appeared to people, I sometimes tell myself, as being something half-baked – or half-formed; as though, perhaps, had I been the offspring of a hen, I had emerged, in error, too quickly from the shell; and was still floundering in an ungainly fashion, in the world in which I had found myself.

Certainly, any form of strong desire; any form of passion; was something quite unknown to me. I seemed to exist more in relation to the desire of others, than to any that existed within myself. I never really longed or pined for anyone; or anything. All that happened to me seemed to happen by chance, not by design. If it hadn't been for Chuck, for example, I know for sure that I would have remained there in that hostel; simply because I lacked the desire to move elsewhere. Not knowing who or what I was, and being, as I say, so half-formed in every respect, it meant that I was lacking in direction; and would never have seen, as Chuck had seen so simply, that because we both so disliked the place, the thing to do was to leave.

One of the respects I mention above, in which I saw myself as being only partially formed, was that of my body. For some reason, I courted the idea that I hadn't yet stopped growing; and that unlike the rest of the human race, I would still grow as the days went by; and that it would perhaps take until I was forty before I would achieve my proper stature. Why that should have been I am not quite sure; but it was the case; so that whenever I saw myself in a mirror, which was seldom (for I had a habit of avoiding all sight of myself) I would be pestered by the impression that it was not myself at all; and that the mirror, in fact, had lied.

However, to provide you with at least *some* kind of picture of how I looked at this time – a picture based upon those rather rare occasions when I *had* dared to observe myself in a glass – I would say that I was of medium height and build, with a pigeon-boned chest, that almost achieved a point: that I had deeply set eyes, that in themselves were dark; largish ears (quite nice ones, I have to admit); and black, or near-black, wispyish kind of hair – with (to make myself at least a little more interesting) a touch of blue in it. In other words, a somewhat nervous, hesitant fledgling, who had not yet learned to fly.

And I was still a virgin; having not as yet had sexual intercourse with any man or woman. Which was quite ridiculous, considering my age; and considering that the majority of men I knew were already fully fledged in that respect – and, it would seem, from how they spoke about themselves, were trying out all sorts of things, with all sorts of people. Which meant that I was something of a freak; and could have been, as I now see, one further reason why Chuck and I had ended up together.

For whilst there was not doubt whatsoever in my mind that Chuck's sexual life was exceedingly active; and that, whether he happened to be screeching off on his motorbike or not, his fantasy, when he was not in the City (and even there too, perhaps – who knows?) was able to focus itself upon the idea that, outside him, in the big wide world, there were others like himself, who shared similar sexual desires; they were none the less desires from which what we call love itself was inevitably excluded.

So that, although we were different in one respect (and as different as well, of course, in our physiques, as chalk is reputed to be from cheese) what Chuck and I had in common – and what, as I now see, had probably drawn us suddenly together – was this lack that existed in the both of us of a capacity for love. Which means that one could say, I suppose (although here, I think, I am being a little harsh towards us both) that we weren't unlike that patient of the analyst who had achieved a transference on to dogs; and that our move into the flat Chuck found in South Kensington, close to the temples of Art and of Science, was in a certain sense an improvement in our condition; in much the same way, I am inclined to imagine, as that transference on to dogs, and so away from public stables, had been for the analyst's patient, a distinct improvement in his.


# II


IT IS BECAUSE I've not written a book before that I have just shown the preceding pages to a friend of mine who is a critic, and who is rather up in literary affairs. And what he has said to me is that whilst what I have set down so far isn't too bad, he thinks, for a beginner, it might help, he said, if I already had the book's title in mind. Some writers actually begin with the title, he told me, and sort of work backwards from there. It might set the real tone for you, he added – whatever that might mean: create a kind of climate: give you a notion, perhaps, he half muttered, of what the book might be about.

Quite frankly, I thought this was rubbish. I mean, surely the title of the book is the very last thing I should be thinking about, since, to me, it's the final putting on of a lid of sorts. However, this, as I say, is quite a literary gent. Someone with words coming out of his eyes and ears, and just about everywhere else as well. So I have decided to give it a whirl, as the Americans say; thinking, in my naive fashion, that finding a title for something must be the easiest thing in the world; and particularly when, as in this case, it has to serve as yet for only a few miserable pages of writing.

So 'Puppy Dog Tales', is what I have thought to myself – how about that? – being, of course, a play upon 'slugs and snails and puppy dogs' tails', which boys are said to be made of; and to emphasise that this is not a book about girls, who are made of 'sugar and spice and all things nice' – or who are said to be, at least.

And yet, to be honest (and if there is one thing I am trying to be, it is that in this book) such a title sounds too twee to me; or too cute, perhaps. So not that then – not 'Puppy Dog Tales': something else has to be found – if, as I say, I am to follow this expert's advice. And he really is an expert. I can assure you of that. I mean, he's read just about everything, from Lao-Tzeu to Baudelaire to Ackerley (one of his favourite authors): *The Discourses of Rumi* is something he goes on about: Breton's *Nadja* – that's a book he's always wanting me to read: the Russians, of course: George Eliot (you should hear him talk about the influence of *her* writing upon Proust, and about how the Grandcourts in *Daniel Deronda* – a couple in the book, I was told – are the precursors of the Guermantes – the Duke and Duchess of, that is). He's good too on *Moby Dick* – a book I have never been able to stomach (if you will please excuse that awful belly of a pun); and also, and in particular, on the early novels of Lawrence (why not the later ones, I don't know); which makes him go on about the need for a writer to have a political stance and that kind of thing: to be committed; a 'committed writer' is how he speaks of him, of Lawrence; as if it isn't a commitment for anyone to take up a piece of paper, and to set down their thoughts upon it, or their feelings – and, perhaps, at times, their more powerful emotions as well. I would have thought that that would be enough of a commitment in itself.

But not for him, it seems – so I suppose I can't consider myself one of those; one of those committed writers; because, to be honest, politics bore me; seeming, as they do to me, to be mere surface symptoms: surface features, as it were, of much deeper things inside. And *that* is what interests me. Not the surface; not the appearance; but what's going on beneath it. Yet, having said that, and having said too that I will be honest, I can hardly see that there is much evidence of it in what I have written down so far. After all, what has there been? A few asides about transvestitism; a brief description of the writer – meaning, myself; and of his flat-mate, called Chuck, Chuckles or Bruce: brief mention of a Scot called George; a little scene about a motorbike and about Chuck dressed up in leather – and that's about it. What's so much beneath the surface about that I would like to know. In fact, I have to ask myself, what's it all about, period?

And funnily enough, that very thought, that very question, has given me an idea (I haven't learned as yet to be chary of *those* you see) which is that my book should be called just that – 'What's It All About?'

Now, that would be as good a handle as any, I'll say to my friend – the one who knows such a lot about literature. Have you ever seen a book called that? – called 'What's It All About?' Sounds good, doesn't it? Will make people want to buy it; and it certainly isn't too cute or too twee, like 'Puppy Dog Tales', which is all curly-wurly. People might even wonder what kind of book it is: whether it is even non fiction, perhaps; in the sense, I mean, of it being maybe a treatise of some kind, upon some high-faluting subject, such as the meaning of the universe; or why we are here; or some such serious-minded subject as that.

Still, having a title of that kind might actually be a hindrance to the sale of the book. I mean, if people took it up, thinking it was something like that, and then started reading, as they would, about men in drag, they could easily get offended: put it down sharply – which is the very opposite of what is required.

So, regarding this famous title, then – which, I have been advised, might be the next thing I should be thinking about; having said to my friend – the literary one – that I wasn't quite sure of how to advance the book; in the sense, that is, of exactly what I should do next (and which is often a bother, it seems, in anything that is creative) – I have heard or read somewhere (I am not quite sure which) that in a work of art (yes, well, that is what I am *intending* this book to be) the element of surprise is what is so important: keeps the reader on his or her toes, and so forth; if that is a suitable expression.

So how about (since it would certainly be surprising) instead of simply calling the book 'What's It All About?' – which, as we have decided, could possibly be misleading; how about our adding an extra word to that: a word, for instance, such as 'Slawomir'?

Now there's a title, it seems to me – 'What's It All About,

Slawomir?' I mean, it's certainly striking – isn't it? – and it is surprising as well, because the reader will have no more idea than I have who Slawomir might be. And it sounds good too. Has a good ring to it. And I can easily see it on the cover of a book, and on its spine as well; even of this one. So I think it will do. And at least it has got me going again – that's the important thing. To have bridged what I sensed was going to be a difficult moment; and to have moved me forward – and onward, into time. For that's what it's all about – life, I mean. Not letting that old, grey-haired thing get the better of you – Time, that is; that old one with the sickle. Maintaining yourself: keeping on top of things: stopping the past from giving you a right old clobbering, as it is wont to do.

I once tried to read Proust, just to see if there was any truth in that idea I told you about the Grandcourts – those two characters in *Daniel Deronda* – but I didn't get very far with it: all those hawthorns in bloom and things. But I could sense that he knew a thing or two about time, and about how the past affects the present and matters of that kind; and I'd certainly like to know how to write something about that. It seems the perfect subject for something modern: to be seeing everything in a state of flux, with nothing solid or really permanent, except the fact of change. That certainly makes sense to me, because when I look back, at what is behind me – at my youth, for example – nothing seems very definite or settled. Things are always dissolving, changing, turning from this into that. And there is so much illusion in life in any case: so much deceit, mask, pretence – not only of the kind that can make a man disguise himself as a woman, but also, as I had seen with Chuck, of the kind that functions within ourselves, in which just one aspect of our being will disguise itself from another.

To give a particular example of this – of the latter, I mean

– not so long ago, I met a young mother of three, who told me, in a most strident manner, that she thought the element of violence in today's cinema quite disgusting; and gave this as a reason for her not going to the cinema at all; out of fear, she told me, of what she might witness. Yet oddly enough, not only did she listen to the most raucous pop music imaginable (which, to my mind, could invoke violence in almost anyone) but also, upon the walls of her rooms, she had hung a set of over-large photographs (truly enormous ones) depicting tough young men on motorbikes (Marlon Brando and the like); and looking, I thought, rather like Chuck, when dressed up in his leathers.

Yet she saw no incongruity in this. 'Oh, that's different,' she said: 'I had them when I was a student.' Yet I cannot help asking myself what effect they will have upon her children; and whether she might not be rearing, albeit unconsciously, a miniature troop of fascists.

However, to get back to where we were in Chapter One; that is, to Chuck and myself in our new abode. And also to George, the clean, good-looking Scot, who occasionally went to our pub.

Why we have to get back to *him* – to George – is because just a few nights after the one I described, when Chuck had shown that he could be jealous, I bumped into him in the street, quite close to our flat.

'Hello, Richard,' he said (for that, reader, is my proper name): 'Nice to see you,' he said. 'Where've you been? How's Chuck?'

I assured him that Chuck was fine, being, that very evening, at his friend Darby's (perhaps you will remember my mentioning that name earlier, when Chuck was about to go off on his motorbike; and how he, Chuck, had told me to say to Darby if he rang, that he had just gone off on his bike.)

'Who's Darby?' asked George, with what I sensed was some kind of tension in his voice.

'Darby? He's a friend of his – or colleague, rather. He works with Chuck in the City.'

'Oh.' There was a pause, and George looked down at me with an impressive, almost abstract stare; then followed it with – 'Sees a lot of people, does he?'

'Who? Chuck? Yes. He does. Sometimes. Quite a few.'

This seemed to answer his question, and there was a further silence. Fronted by those marvellous features of his, and his opaque, near-white complexion, I had no idea of what his thoughts might be; yet his remoteness in no way disturbed me; and I recall thinking to myself, as we stood there in that busy London street, that we had become locked together in some peculiar mental space: a space that seemed to extend itself beyond us; and for some considerable distance.

'So what are you doing?' – George broke the silence.

'Doing?' I answered, again unable to fathom him.

'Yes – doing. Right now. This very moment.'

I wanted to reply, knowing how very logical he was, that I was standing right there in the street – talking to him; but said instead – 'I'm on my way home.'

'Oh,' said George again, allowing a further silence to accrue. Then, with what I can only describe as being a great heavy lurch of his voice, he added, 'Come to the pub. I'll treat you. Come for a drink, Richard; a wee glass of something.'

To be honest, I cannot recall how I responded to this request; but whatever words I used, I know that just a short while later, we were tucked away in a corner of the bar, with pint-sized glasses on the table; and George was telling me about his girl – who, he said, was about to ditch him.

'You know about girls, Richard?' he asked.

'Hardly,' I replied.

'How do you mean – hardly?' he asked, in his very logical manner.

'Well,' I said, being honest, 'I've never had one.'

'Never had a girl! A wee lass!' he exclaimed, showing for once a degree of emotion. 'Don't give me that, Richard.'

'Well, I haven't,' I said, with what I felt was a blush; though I don't think that it showed.

'Oh, Richard' – his pale grey eyes seemed almost to stare at me. 'Richard,' he repeated; and staring in that manner, again fell into silence.

And in that silence we remained for some time, sipping away at our drinks, oblivious of all that was around us: of the steadily filling bar; of the gradual build-up of 'good evenings' to the barmaid, as the locals made their way in; and of the buzz beyond the curtained window where we sat of London's heavy traffic.

Here, perhaps, I need to make an interjection, in order to enlarge a little upon something I said earlier about Chuck and myself, and our incapacity for love. I don't believe too much in cause and effect, but because they are trained to it, a lot of people do these days, it seems; which is why no doubt they are always saying such things as that it is because they were bashed over the head when they were young, that they are in the state they are in today; and which, in a way, to me seems somewhat irreligious. Irreligious, I mean, in the sense that it supposes that everything can be explained away; whereas, as I've grown older, I have come to see things more in terms of us having some kind of story of our own to tell: one that we have to live out – whatever may have happened to us in the past, or might be happening to us today – or, indeed, may happen to us in the future. Of course, we may 'use' the things that happen to us, to help us uncover the story, and to give our life meaning by that method; but it's the story that counts, is how I see it: the myth, so to speak, that is really governing our lives.

Not following that latter idea, however, it could be said, I daresay, that one of the dominant features of my life is the fact that I was abandoned as a child; and that I grew up, as a result, without the closeness of parents. Not that I was adopted, because I was simply placed in care; and my very earliest memories are those of being with a bevy of similar children in a 'home'; and of my being obliged to share with them, as substitute parent-figures, a master and a matron.

Now, whether or not that was a *reason* for my condition, I cannot say (the condition, as I have described it, of being unable to love). But there are scores of people who would assure me that it has to be the case; and who, if told, would say knowingly that it explains it. 'Poor thing,' they would utter, in a rather condescending manner, 'you weren't loved, like other children – and so, of course, you aren't able to love in return.' And I have to admit that in one way at least it seems difficult to go against that. Difficult, that is, if it weren't for the fact that, as far as I know, none of the other children in that home suffered a similar inhibition as they grew up; nor, for that matter, does it explain the condition of Chuck, who had been reared by parents who adored him.

And certainly, I was never treated badly in that home. I may not have been cosseted and cuddled, and may not have experienced that kind of animal closeness, experienced by other children, of being in bed at times with those who brought them up. But I was never beaten. The master did use a stick on occasions, it is true; but it was reserved for only extreme cases of rebellion and the like; and in any case, only for the older boys: so if I lacked, as I say, the closeness of animal warmth, I in no way lacked the experience of kindness and of care – and of decency too, and orderliness;

which, when one considers the emotional savagery of what appears to be most people's family lives, ought, surely, to have stood me in good stead; and in some ways to have made it easier for me to draw near to other people.

Also, regarding my sexuality – which, of course, as I had seen with Chuck, didn't have to depend upon love in order to flourish – my lack of parents, and my having been brought up in a home, could hardly account for my inhibitions in that respect; for sex there was rampant: not in the form of intercourse (or certainly not as far as I was concerned), but in that of mutual masturbation, which was indulged in nightly by the older boys (and often during the daytime as well) either in bed or in the toilets – or even in the street, on dark winter evenings – perhaps after church, which we were encouraged to go to on our own when we were older; or even, as I remember, at the hairdresser's, where once, as I was waiting to be given a quick 'short back and sides' (barbers were brusque in those days) a young assistant, on the pretence of asking me to help him remove some boxes to a back room, had there unbuttoned me, and had delivered me in seconds: and this with the door between the two half open, and with that kind of awed silence beyond, that seemed to be such a feature of hairdressers' parlours – of male ones, that is; broken only by the occasional whirr of the electric clippers – or (for barbers still used them in those days) the flat, steady sound of an open razor being stropped.

Not that I want this book of mine to be one of those drop-your-trousers books as I think of them, which go into such detail about their characters' sexual habits; and which, however dressed up they may be with literary embellishments and the like, cannot resist titillating the reader at each twist and turn of the page. It just isn't – *can't* be – that type of book; simply because I, myself, never really think like that.

I am not a prude; and no-one enjoys more than I do a good touch of the old slap and tickle in a book, or a bit of hot, salacious writing. I really do think, for instance, that *Lady Chatterley's Lover* is a most marvellous work of art: rich, resplendent, exotic, and with vine leaves in its hair; and why people should have gone against it so is beyond me; unless it is again that phoniness of the Victorians, which had lingered on in them.

My story then – my personal one, that is – whatever the cause of it may be, had gradually led me to a position where I had no close physical contact with anyone; and after a certain moment in my late teens, even that form of sexual relief I have just spoken about had suddenly come to an end; and as yet, I had not found any other form; in the way, for instance, that Chuck had done; and of which, until I met him, I really did know nothing.

Not that I was at all embarrassed by this. I certainly didn't think of it as a problem. For me, it seemed that this was a stage through which I was meant to pass; and I gained as much pleasure from thinking about people, as I did from touching them in any intimate sort of way: which is why I was so curious about George, as we sat there in that pub together; wondering why he should have told me about his girl; why he had asked me questions about Chuck and about myself; and why it was that I was so unable to fathom him, and to see what lay beyond that remote cool stare of his. Was he, perhaps, I wondered, in some way as cut off from people as I was? Was his story, the one that he was being forced to live out, in part, perhaps, a reflection of my own? Why was his girl about to ditch him? was another thought that came into my head (he had said nothing further about that); and why had he more or less dragged me to where we were sitting, in a corner of that bar, with freshly filled glasses between us, and with our heads beginning to spin?

'Richard.' George's voice was a trifle blurred, I noticed.

'Yes?' I replied, guessing that mine must have been the same.

'Do you know what, Richard?'

I didn't answer this.

'Do you know what?' he went on, leaning towards me, 'You keep reminding me of someone.'

'Do I, George?' I replied.

'Yes, you do,' he said, 'you remind me of –'; he then paused: 'You know who you remind me of, Richard? You – oh –'

George's voice trailed away, and his eyes appeared to turn inward; in much the same way, I remember noticing, as Chuck's had done, when he had first appeared before me in his gear. Then suddenly, and as his eyes again came into focus, he said –

'Richard. What would you say if I came back to the flat with you? Chuck's not there,' he said, ' – is he? What do you say – eh; about my coming back to the flat with you?'

For once I found myself panicking. In spite of the alcohol inside me, my mind made agile leaps of various kinds; thinking to itself, why does George want to come back to the flat with me? What if I say yes and if Chuck should be there? What will Chuck say – do? Will he be jealous; and if so, of what? Do I want this – whatever it might be? Bells were ringing noisily in my head, signalling that here, suddenly, my story might be about to change. Had George formed a projection upon me; and was that the reason why he had asked about Chuck; about his habits and his friends? And if he had, was he aware of that projection, and had I perhaps encouraged it? And if I had, what was *I* wanting from him – from George? Some kind of closeness? Some kind of intimacy? And one that would be quite different from the one that I shared with Chuck – because, as I could

already see, it was so much more direct: because I was no
'Bobo' figure for him – just plain Richard; and because he
hadn't assumed anything, in the way that Chuck had
assumed almost everything, and because he had made this
approach towards me step by step.

'I can't ask you back to the hostel – can I?' George said.
'You know what it's like there, Richard. You can't easily
have anyone with you in your room, without their knowing. You remember – don't you – how it was . . .? Look, if
Chuck *should* be at the flat,' he said, 'I'll just say – well, I'll
just say something about having met you in the street; and
that I wanted to call and say hello to him. You know how
Chuck is, Richard,' he said, 'he likes attention; to be
flattered . . . Come on,' he said, rising from his seat. 'drink
up. Let's go. I know where it is' (meaning the flat), 'I went
there when you first moved in; just to see how it was. Come
on – drink up. Let's go. We'll be plastered if we stay on here
much longer.'

And with that command, I stood up, drank up, and
obediently followed George out of the pub; feeling that
suddenly things were out of my hands: that George's will,
drive, desire was stronger than my own; and that if, by
chance, it should prove necessary, he could more than cope
with Chuck, which was a persistent source of worry to me.

The flat, as you must have gathered, was only a short
distance away, and I have no memory of that brief walk we
made together on that dark winter evening in South
Kensington: nor of our climbing the stairs: nor of my letting
us in – which I must have done, since it was I who had the
key. All I can see is George quickly making himself at home,
once he had made sure that Chuck wasn't there; and his
swiftly filling a kettle in the kitchen and putting it on to boil:
then muttering something about us having a mug of coffee,

in order to make us both more sober – which, in a way, I remember telling myself, was the last thing that I wanted – to be that; to be more sober; for the relaxation I was then experiencing was something entirely new to me; and for a while, I realised, had been gradually drawing me out of myself.

I was vaguely aware, however, that the most pressing question at the back of my drunken mind was the one of whether George was in some way in love with me; and that if this should be so – for that is how I thought of it – there was the threat of a real change in my life: a threat, I mean, because, after all, one does rather cling to one's habits; and I had avoided all forms of emotional involvement for some years (as I say, since soon after my teens): and as I was now in my twenties, it seemed a very long time indeed.

'Where's the coffee?' asked George, as the kettle came to the boil. 'Richard,' he almost shouted at me, as I lingered in my room, collapsing swiftly into a chair beside my bed.

'The coffee,' I answered, somewhat stupidly. 'It's there; on the shelf' (this was said in a very vague sort of way), 'above the sink; above the draining-board.'

'Found it,' came the reply. 'Sugar for you?' he went on, as he stepped for a moment out of the kitchen. 'Sugar, Richard?'

I don't know what, or if, I answered. All I can remember is that as he stood there looking at me, George suddenly burst into laughter: a laughter that was totally unexpected – mainly because I couldn't help noticing that his voice, which was usually rather heavy, suddenly became curiously light in tone – almost silly, in fact.

'Richard – you're drunk,' George said, as he came across to me. 'You're a wee bit tipsy – aren't you?' he added, as he swiftly knelt beside my chair. 'Eh – aren't you?' he repeated – and with that, stretched out one of those long, bony hands of his, upon which the flesh was thick enough to give an extra impression of strength, and with it began steadily stroking my thigh.

The effect of this was quite startling; because I suddenly felt something that I had not felt before in my life – a kind of trembling in my body that at first provoked a kind of shiver; and then, as George persisted, transformed itself into a steady glow of warmth. It was a feeling so new to me, and so unknown, that I remember wishing that we could stay like that forever; that George and I could remain there in that position for days, months – even for years. But no sooner had I thought that thought, than the kettle began to whistle (do whistling kettles still exist, I wonder?) and, at the same time (how curiously synchronistic such things can be at times) we both became conscious of a different sound altogether: that of a key being turned in a door; and both of us knew, then, in a flash, that Chuck had just come home; and was about to enter the room.

I must say that George's mental and physical skill impressed me enormously at that moment; for not only did he swiftly retreat to the kitchen, leaving me sprawling upon my chair; he also had sufficient sense and presence of mind to call out to Chuck as he came in.

'Is that you, Chuck?' he asked, in a half serious tone, as Chuck stepped through the main entrance door; and as he himself, at the same time, stepped neatly out of the kitchen. 'Richard is drunk, I'm afraid. I met him at the pub. I was just making him some coffee.'

From my position in the chair, which was almost opposite the door, I could clearly see Chuck's reaction to this; how, with a grand, almost imperious stare, he turned his eyes first towards George, and then towards myself; quickly assessing the situation: expressing little or no surprise; allowing his mind to take in what was before him – and then, having done that, bringing things quickly under his control.

'*Well*,' Chuck said to me, in an almost motherly kind of voice, 'what's this all about then, Richard?' (He avoided using the name Bobo, I noticed.) 'Had a few too many – have you? George got you drunk – did he?'

I knew instinctively that I should avoid any defence of George, and merely shook my head in a non-committal manner; feeling confident that George would make no blunder. And I was proved right about this, for he quickly said to Chuck, 'I think he'd had a few before I met him, Chuck. I didn't realise –'

'Well, it doesn't *matter*,' Chuck said to him: then called out to me, in the way that a hen might call out to its chick, 'It doesn't matter – does it, Richard; now that your Auntie Zee is here?' and with that, let out one of those bouncy, frothy giggles of his. 'George has made some *coffee* for you, Richard,' he went on, as though I hadn't heard a word that he had said, and which was partly my own fault, I thought, since I had answered as yet to nothing. 'And it's very *nice* of him – do you *hear*, Richard? – It's very *nice* of George.' Then, turning to George, and speaking, I thought, in a somewhat confidential manner, as though he and George were in league with each other (and which was his way, I suppose, of keeping things under his control) he said, 'We'd better give him the coffee; and then, I think, he'd be best off in his bed.'

George nodded and disappeared: then reappeared. 'Does he take sugar?' he asked. 'One,' said Chuck sharply. 'Just one.'

George nodded again, and disappeared into the kitchen a second time; and Chuck stood looking at me with what I took to be a reproving kind of smile. Then, as George handed him the coffee (for which, I noticed, he expressed no form of thanks) he came across to me. 'Here's your coffee, Richard,' he said, speaking in a commanding fashion, and forcing me to pull myself together. '*Drink* it,' he said; 'then we're getting you off to bed.'

I sat up – up straight, that is; and as I took the coffee from him, I remember muttering something to the effect that anyone would think that I was drunk. 'Well, you are,' Chuck said. 'You are, Richard – you're pissed. Isn't he, George? You're pissed, Richard,' he went on, letting out another of his giggles.

And then as I sat there, sipping away at that steaming mug of coffee; with Chuck standing over me, and with him willing me to finish it; I risked allowing my eyes to cross quickly to the kitchen doorway, where I knew somehow that George would still be lingering. And by some means or another – one that seemed close to that of telepathy – managed to convey to him the message that it might be best if he were to leave. And sure enough, as if it were a proof that we had bridged some kind of barrier – a barrier which, I was to learn later, was important to us both – George responded to it rapidly, and with skill.

'Chuck,' he said to Chuck, 'you don't need my help, do you, with the wee bairn?' (He seemed to know by some kind of instinct that I would be in no way offended by that expression, and would realise that he was using it only as a means of dealing with Chuck.) 'I was on my way home.'

'Oh, no,' replied Chuck, without turning, and with a kind of greediness in his voice, 'we don't need *George* – do we Bobo?' (He had now slipped back into his use of my nickname, I noticed.) 'We don't need to bother wee Georgie *any more* – do we, Bobo?' he repeated, with an emphasis upon both the any and the more.

'Well, I'll be off then,' George answered quickly. 'See you, Richard,' he called out to me. 'See you, Chuck,' he wisely added. And then, with a swift glance in my direction – too swift, I am afraid, for me to see what meaning it contained – he left; closing the door of the flat behind him. And doing it in such a manner, I should add, as to make it quite obvious to us both that his departure was not a permanent one; and that before much time had elapsed, he would be entering our life again.

# III

YOU WILL NOW be wondering, I expect, what happened next; after George had left the flat: whether Chuck had made a scene, perhaps, and how I eventually got to bed. So rather than indulge in one of those asides I seem to be so fond of, I'd better get down to that immediately. After all, there's nothing like a good old bit of story-telling to help a book along. This modern habit we have of chopping everything up into teeny bits and pieces may reflect the fragmented view we have of things these days, and can be pertinent, I suppose, on account of that; but there's still nothing better – is there – than a good old yarn, when the interest might be flagging: as it could be right now, with my having pushed my luck with the first two chapters of this book, and with my wanting to push it further. The Victorians certainly knew their onions in that respect: in the respect, I mean, of knowing how to spin a good tale; keeping all sorts of things up their sleeves; such as a new character appearing unexpectedly and so on. Dickens was good at that – at surprises; and so were the Brontës – Charlotte in particular; like having that mad woman locked up in a cupboard – or room, rather: then getting out of it at night, and setting fire to the place; and causing Jane to go off in a huff, because she hadn't known that this big Bertha of a woman was the mad wife of her lover.

So – to go on with the story; *our* story, that is . . . After George had left the flat, Chuck checked to see that the entrance door had been properly locked; then bolted it, as he did each night; came back into the room; removed his jacket; flung it upon the bed; slipped his hands beneath his braces; and then began to rub them across his chest in a noticeably agitated fashion.

'Now – you listen to me, Bobo,' he said, once he had calmed himself a little. 'You just listen to your Auntie Zee . . . Do you *hear* me, Bobo?' he asked insistently, leaning slightly over me. 'You are going to *listen*: to Chuckles,' he said. 'Words of good advice,' he said. 'Right *now* – however pissed you might be' – and with that, sat down upon my bed; quite close to the chair in which I was sitting – or sprawling, rather.

'You're going to speak to me about George – aren't you?' I asked, sensing that I needed some quick form of defence.

'Am I?' he asked. 'What makes you think that? What makes you think I'm going to do that?'

'I don't know,' I answered, 'I – '

'Yes, well I *am*,' he went on: 'You just keep away from him, Bobo: that's what I'm telling you.' He was breathing, I noticed, in a curious manner, drawing his breath in through his nose and puffing himself out, so that he looked enormous. 'You're going to get hurt, Bobo – *that's* what's going to happen. I know his type. I've met 'em before: talking about girls and things. He's just a big Scotch blond with frostbite – that's what he is. A fag, Bobo. A real old fag. Do you hear me, Bobo? And he's after you. I knew it when I came in.'

By now he had risen to his feet again, and was pacing about the room. 'He just doesn't know what he wants, Bobo – that's the truth of it. He's got a big, fat cock, I suspect, and can't think where to put it. That's *his* trouble. He's not like us, Bobo – do you hear? Not like Bobo and his Auntie Zee. He's a real phoney – do you hear that? . . . He'll trick you – that's what he'll do. Pretend he's in love with you. Get you all messed up – and then he'll piss off; leave you, Bobo, as if nothing had *happened*.'

'Chuck,' I asked, not much affected by what he was saying, 'what's a fag?'

'What's a *what*!' Chuck exclaimed.

'A fag. You said George was a fag.'

'Now you look here, young man,' he said (he had never called me that before), 'don't come that stuff with *me*; as if you didn't know what *that* means. I thought better of you than that, Bobo. Never thought you'd play the innocent . . . So don't tell me you don't know what a fag is. Don't say it to me, Bobo. I'm not *playing* with you – I'm *telling* you; for real. You've had the gipsy's warning – do you hear that? Do you hear me, Bobo; what I have said?'

I nodded as if to say yes.

'Well then,' Chuck continued, 'if you've really *heard* me, Bobo; I want you to make a promise: make your Auntie Zee a promise: that you'll keep away from him – from George. Now; are you going to do that, or not? Are you, now?'

I nodded again, feeling that a sudden tiredness was about to come over me.

'Well, I'm glad you *are*,' said Chuck, letting out a great blast of air, 'I'm very pleased to hear it. No more of that Georgie-Porgie stuff. No more of him about the place. That's a promise now – isn't it? It's for your own *good*, Bobo. It's not for mine. I don't want you to get hurt – that's all. Those bastards are good at that – at making you suffer. I *know*, Bobo. Take my word for it. I've seen a lot of them. A *lot* of them – do you hear?' He paused – then added sharply,

'Now then: it's time to get you to bed. I just hope you've taken it in – that's all. I'm not going to go over it again, you know. It's not *me* to do that. I've said my piece, Bobo – and you've heard it, I hope. Now it's time for bed – for bye-byes.'

By this time I was half asleep; and Chuck, seeing that this was so, came quickly across the room to give me a shake.

'Oh, come on, Bobo,' he said. 'Wake up! Wakey, wakey!' – and with that, caught hold of me and sat me upon my bed. 'Now then,' he went on, 'can you undress yourself, or not . . . or are you too far gone?' he asked; 'too non-compos mentis?'

My eyes opened widely at this remark, never having heard Chuck use it before, and because his doing so had given me a quick, new view of his person.

'You are, I see,' he said, as he swiftly removed my jacket and then my shirt, and pushed me back on to the bed.

'I'll do the rest, Chuck,' I managed to utter: 'I'm okay – I promise you . . .'

'Promise me *nothing*,' Chuck replied sharply. 'You're pissed, Bobo – that's what you are; *pissed*'; and with that, slipped off my shoes, undid my belt, and swiftly removed my trousers.

I don't quite know why, but at this point I started to panic. Was it, perhaps, because I had never undressed myself in front of Chuck before – or, rather, been undressed *by* him; and that a strong feeling of shyness then came over me? Whatever, I remember how I then squirmed about on the bed, unable to do very much – even to raise myself on to my elbows; which only encouraged Chuck the more.

'Oh, Bobo, Bobo!' he said, laughing at my predicament. 'You really are pissed, aren't you? Really, really *pissed*!' – and upon that remark, let out one of those hefty, bouncy giggles of his; picked me up; deftly removed my vest; threw me over his shoulder; and pushed my pants down over my bottom.

So there I was – drunk; and naked as on the day when I was born; and caught in the arms of my Auntie Zee. I cannot say that I was covered in shame, for I was much too drunk to be that. And I cannot say that Chuck was in any way discourteous to me. He didn't make fun of me at that moment, as he might have done, I thought. I don't remember that he even looked at me. Instead, he flicked my pyjamas out from beneath my pillow; and then, still holding me in his arms, with my head flopped over his shoulder, he slipped on the trousers, pulled them up to my waist, rolled me back on to the bed, took the trouser cord and tied it, picked me up again, thrust my arms, one by one, into the sleeves of the pyjama jacket, pushed back my hair, which had fallen over my eyebrows; and then, with one gigantic movement (he really impressed me with that) drew down the sheets and the blankets, and popped me into my bed.

'Now,' he said, speaking authoritatively, and striding across to a light-switch, 'you'd better get yourself to sleep . . . Better sleep on it . . . Do you *hear* me, Bobo?' he almost shouted, 'Chuckles is going to bed.'

'I hear you, Chuck,' I murmured, my head now deep in my pillow, 'I can hear you, Chuck.'

'Well, goodnight then,' he answered, as he switched off the light, '– and sleep tight.'

But before I could hear more, I had fallen into my dreams; and Chuck and George and the flat, as well as those lofty Victorian palaces, with which I had by now become so familiar, were as unreal to me as the world itself, to which they only partially belonged; and I was in some different place and time; where the mess and jumble of the day is hastily reassembled; and where those gnomelike nannies of the underworld are picking away at our brains: sifting them, sorting them – tidying them; making them ready for the morning.

I shall now have to digress for a moment, because I want to get back to the Victorians. They really knew – didn't they? – (their writers, I mean) how to get a real swell going in their books, and how to carry the story forward to an ending, and beyond it to another; and then, if necessary, to a further ending again. They had no shame about that – about keeping the reader guessing, and using all sorts of tricks and devices, such as undiscovered wills and things like that; or lost relatives, who suddenly turn up out of the past. And in their language too, they could get a good swell going there; making it rich and resonant; and they had no shame about that either – not in the way we would have today. I mean, we couldn't write something such as Charlotte Brontë wrote about Big Bertha, as I have called her, the woman locked in a cupboard (why do I keep using that word?) in *Jane Eyre*. We couldn't write something like, 'What crime was this, that lived incarnate in this sequestered mansion? What mystery, that broke out, now in fire and now in blood, at the deadest hours of night?' – we wouldn't dare. Yet you have to admit that it gives a powerful effect; mostly, I think, because you kind of sense somehow that she – Charlotte – isn't speaking about a 'person' at all, but about something so much larger than that: some figure – some symbol, perhaps, of how Time can work its revenge; at any moment, and upon anyone. How, just when you're thinking that everything's hunky-dory, and that all in the garden is lovely, something springs out at you from the past, and gives you a right old bashing.

Or that is what she seems to be to me – Big Bertha; or Grace Poole's charge, as I sometimes think of her (Grace being the woman who had charge of her in that cupboard) –

39

a symbol of how so much in us is stored away: forgotten, or seemingly forgotten; until suddenly, it breaks free – and wham! – Jane is sent reeling across the moors; knocking on people's doors at night; crying for help – for shelter; seeking the refuge of a tight-lipped, do-gooder parson, to get her out of her troubles.

Not, let me hasten to add, that I thought something like that was likely to happen to *me*. I don't mean by that that I considered myself to be above such things – no-one can be that; but that, unlike most of the human race, I had no past at all to catch up with me – or none, at least, that I knew of. Because I told you – didn't I? – that my parents had abandoned me; as a child; as a baby, in fact: dumped me upon the steps of a police station, or so I gathered; with no indication of who I was, or where I had come from. And that's not a nice thing to have happen to anyone; not to know who your parents are: not even their name: nothing. It leaves you with a dreadful hole inside yourself; a great gap; with no possibility of having it filled. Sometimes, I would say to myself that I'd put an advertisement in the papers – or, rather, in the paper of the small town where I had been found; referring to the date and time at which some burly police constable had discovered me; and asking my parents – or parent (there might have been just one, I suppose) – would they please mind stepping forward and presenting themselves to me; so that I would have a mum and a dad (or at least one of the two) like everybody else.

And I often pictured what might happen. How, out of the blue, I would receive a letter or note, sent c/o the paper, and using the box number it had provided, saying something like I am your long lost mother, or father – or both; and asking forgiveness for what they had done. And then there'd be this scene – wouldn't there? – where I'd turn up at Claridge's, or somewhere like that, and learn that I was the son of a duchess or something – or, conversely, that I would prove to be the opposite; and my parents just a couple of rough old soaks, that I'd be meeting at Clapham Junction; and who, having replied to that advertisement in the paper, were only after me for my money: which, because I really didn't have any right then, made for a sorry ending to my tale, with everyone grim and grey and rather ugly.

About ten days after that scene in the flat, when Chuck had sent George packing and had tucked me up in my bed, Chuck decided (in that way he had of deciding almost everything) that what I was urgently in need of was a breath of good, fresh air; and that nothing else would explain my ghastly pallor.

'You need to get out of the place,' he said; 'you read too much.' (It was true that I read a lot, but mostly detective stories, I am afraid.) 'You're coming to the sea,' he said, 'to visit my aunt ... to Bognor,' he said. 'We'll go on Saturday,' he said. 'We'll stay the night,' he said.

I don't think for a moment that Chuck associated the state I was in – the general wanness of my complexion, and the fact that I was off my food – with my not having seen or heard from George. With Chuck, once a thing was done it was done. In *his* mind, George had been banished from our world; and as far as *my* mind was concerned, I had promised to do the same. But I had not been able to keep that promise, alas; because as the hours and days had gone by, I couldn't help thinking of him; seeing that cool, steady gaze of his peering down at me in the bar; or experiencing that unexpected glow of warmth, as he had knelt beside me in my chair. Yet I lacked the confidence to act – to actually *do* something; such as telephone George at the hostel (I did know that there was a pay-phone on the stairs); or drop him a note, perhaps – or even go to the pub, as I might have done, in the hope of finding him there. Instead, I had sort of sulked; stayed in; read; nursed my sores. And each day I nurtured the thought that George might call at our door; or might ring, perhaps; for I was sure that he had our number.

Within an hour of his having planned our little excursion to the sea, Chuck was on the phone to Bognor Regis; ringing his aunt – or his aunt's house, rather; for being part bedridden, she herself never answered the phone.

'Jack?' he said (I wondered who Jack was), 'It's Bruce (that was his real name, you will remember). 'How's old Dodo?' (was Dodo his aunt, I wondered; and was it from her perhaps that I had acquired my nickname?) 'Oh, is she!' Chuck went on. 'Naughty girl. Well, you tell her from me, Jack, that she'd better have kicked it by the weekend . . . Why? . . . Well, because I'm coming *down* – that's why . . . Yes . . . No; just for one night – on Saturday . . . There's no-one coming – is there? Not Molly or any-one? . . . No . . . Well, she'll be glad to see me then.' (He laughed at something Jack said) . . . 'I expect you will – poor Jack. Well, you'll tell me all about it. I'm bringing a friend . . . Yes . . . He shares the flat with me . . . Yes . . . No, we *aren't* – why . . .? Oh, that will be alright. *He* won't mind – or I don't think he will' (he said this with a quick giggle) . . . 'He's a bit – you know, "green" . . . But he's *very sweet*. You'll like him, I'm sure. Old Dodo will too. She likes little ones, as *you well know*. Ha, ha! Yes - I know, Jack. You do as well – the younger the better – isn't it? Ha, ha!' (Chuck had turned to look at me) . . . 'No,' he then said, in reply to some question, 'I don't think I can . . . Dark hair? – Yes . . . No . . . ! Ha, ha . . . ! Well, you'll have to see. We'll be there in time for lunch. Tell Bridget. She likes having guests – doesn't she? Sick, poor thing, she must be, of making all those endless cups of Bovril . . . Yes: Saturday . . . Oh, about eleven, I expect. We'll ring you from the station . . . Will you?' he said. 'Thanks, Jack. Give my love to dear old Dodo. Tell her I'm looking forward to seeing her; and Richard is to meeting her . . . Yes – his name . . . Yes – Richard . . . Bye, then – Bye-ee! See you on Saturday. Yes. Elevenish . . . Yes – we *will*. Don't worry.'

'I was just ringing my aunt,' said Chuck, once he had replaced the receiver. 'She's having one of her turns. Been on the bottle, I suspect. But we can go. I've fixed it for Saturday.'

'Who's Jack?' I asked.

'Jack? He's her odd-job-man-cum-chauffeur. Drives her about in an old Rover. He's marvellous. Does everything for her. Dotes on her. He's going to meet us at the station.'

'And what won't I mind, Chuck?' I enquired.

'Mind?'

'Yes. You said I wouldn't mind something.'

'*Did* I?'

'Yes. You said –'

'– Oh, of course; yes. It's nothing, Richard. We'll have to share a room – that's all; a bed. Jack asked if you'd mind. The old dear's been wetting herself again. All that booze, I expect; and there's a shortage of sheets. So he asked if we'd mind sharing.'

'Ah,' I said, not being sure how to reply to this.

'I'd better warn you,' said Chuck, 'Dodo's stone deaf – or almost; and she's got an ear-trumpet that she keeps stuffing into one ear. But she's an old dear: a real trouper,' he said. 'You'll like her.'

'We could take sheets from here, Chuck,' I suggested.

'– No, silly. We don't want to be bothered with that. You don't mind – do you? – sharing a bed with me. I'm not going to *rape* you, Bobo,' he said with a giggle, ' – if *that's* what you're thinking.'

'Don't be stupid, Chuck,' I said a little tetchily; not really liking it when Chuck spoke in this fashion. 'I just thought that – well, that *you* mightn't like it – that's all.'

'Me? Why do you say that?' Chuck expressed some surprise.

'I don't know. I just –'

'Well – it's true: I'm not used to it. But we're sort of *brothers* – aren't we? It's not going to *hurt* us – is it? – to be sharing a bed for once.'

And I felt there was no way in which I could reply to this remark; for Chuck's expression at that moment was so full of genuine care, of such true kindness, that I did in fact half feel that it might be close to brotherly love; and that buried inside him, somewhere beneath that monstrous Auntie Zee figure, through which he would generally relate, was this smaller, neater, more brotherly one; of whom, if we trod carefully, I might eventually grow fond.

Jack was already waiting for us at the station, and there was no need for Chuck to telephone. 'There you are,' he said to us twice, as we stepped on to the platform; and as I saw approaching us this wiry man of about fifty, with wavy, gingerish hair that fitted his head closely; and which, for some reason, I imagined might be false.

'I'll take that,' said Jack, once we had been introduced to each other; and with that swiftly snatched the small grip I was carrying out of my hand, and marched off with Chuck towards the car: which seemed an unnecessary action (snatching the grip, I mean) since it only contained my pyjamas; a toothbrush and paste; a razor, soap, two packets of wine-gums (to help me with my smoking); and the detective novel I was reading just then; and which, as soon as I had finished it, I had promised to give to Chuck.

'How are you, Jack?' asked Chuck, once we had reached the Rover, and were installed in our seats; with Chuck sitting in front. 'How's Dodo?' he said 'How's Bridget? How's the cat?'

'Okay,' said Jack, as we drove off. 'We're all fine. Old Dodo's been on the bottle again, as I expect you gathered – but we're fine. Much the same as always.'

There was nothing particular about what he was saying; but what fascinated me about him, and that I could see clearly in the rear-view mirror, was the way in which his eyes kept dancing about: never seeming to be still at all: checking each small movement that he made: watching Chuck: looking at me occasionally.

'Been to Bognor before, Richard?' he asked.

'Course not,' said Chuck, before I had time to reply, 'never seen the sea before in his life – have you, Richard?' – he teased.

'Oh, I expect he *has*,' said Jack. 'Seen the sea and seen a sailor too, I expect – isn't that so, Richard?' His eyes were jogging merrily as he said this. 'All the nice girls love a sailor – don't they, Chuck?' he said with a bright tinkle in his voice. 'Isn't that so, Richard?' And he said this in such a manner that I felt it would have been mean of me at that moment if I had shown offence at that remark; and that behind all this jaunty play, that was going on between him and Chuck, there was a real decency of feeling – both for me, and for my being such a newcomer to what for them was so familiar; that is to say, to Jack taking care of Chuck's old aunt, in the surprisingly roomy Edwardian villa that we were now approaching by the sea.

For some reason – I suppose because of what Jack had said on the phone about the sheets; about there being a shortage of them, I mean; and which you may remember he had given as being the reason for Chuck and I sharing a bed; I had formed a half-picture in my mind of Aunt Dodo's room:

45

seeing it as something dark and dingy and rather dungeon-like, and smelling somewhat of urine.

It proved, however, to be quite the opposite of that; for being placed upon the first floor of the house, and upon the side of it that overlooked the sea, it was bright and spacious and airy: its colours, if I may use a musical term, being a kind of symphony in silvers, greens and creams. The creams being those of her various bedcovers and linens (we found her in a huge bed close to the window, sitting propped upright against her pillows); and of a heavy, crocheted shawl that she had cast around her shoulders; as well as those of the colours of the walls and general paintwork, and of the room's carpet too, I think: and also, I seem to recall, of some rather attractive lacelike pieces of drapery that covered two or three largish, circular tables that were placed about the room and that gave it an air of distinction.

As for the greens. They were those of a number of healthy-looking plants that had been placed in a series of stocky, Chinese-style pots; either on the draped, circular tables, or in similar pots on the mantelpiece; or in yet smaller ones along the window-sill; and on a tall, elegant table by her bed.

And the silvers? – well, they were partly those of the colour of her hair, which swept back magnificently from her forehead, in two large generous sweeps: in much the same way, I noticed, as Chuck's did from his; and also of an incredible number of photo-frames, of the self-standing variety, that were displayed about the room, and that contained, I quickly remarked, images of what seemed to be 'persons of the theatre'; actresses and actors, with their names scrawled large across the bottom, in the way they do those things; and several of a plump, youngish-looking woman I thought in some way resembled Chuck.

'Brucey! Brucey!' Chuck's aunt called out as we entered the room, and as Chuck went forward to embrace her, taking her into his arms and giving her a hefty kiss on the cheek. 'How *glad* I am to see you,' she boomed at him. 'I never see *anyone!*' she cried out, with a laugh. 'Not these days,' she said.

Chuck was now standing back from the bed and holding her hands in his. 'You're the only friend I've got, Brucey,' she said, looking at him with her great saucer-sized eyes, that were soft and wet at the edges.

'Now, Dodo – don't exaggerate,' said Chuck, mouthing the words carefully. 'Molly was here last *month*. I *know*. Jack told me.'

'*Who?*' she shouted, taking up her ear-trumpet, and placing it in one ear.

'Molly,' said Chuck, now lowering his voice a little.

'Oh, Molly,' she said. 'She only comes here when she wants to wash her knickers: *that's* the trouble with her,' she said. 'And she gets Jack and Bridget to do it for her – that's what makes me cross, you know . . . Who's this?' she suddenly asked, as her eyes crossed the room to where I was lingering in the background.

'Ah,' said Chuck, beckoning me forward. 'This is Richard.'

'Who?'

'Rich-ard,' said Chuck. 'He's my *friend*.'

'O-oh!' answered Chuck's aunt, in what I thought was a suggestive manner.

'He shares the *flat* with me.'

'O-oh,' she repeated. 'Does he now . . .? Well, I'm very pleased to meet you, young man,' she said, in a forthright manner, stretching out her hand; which, as I clasped it, I found to be surprisingly warm; with its soft, plump flesh pressing through its thin, papery skin.

'What does he do?' asked the aunt; looking at me, but speaking to Chuck.

'He's an estate agent,' said Chuck (which wasn't true). 'He works near Harrods,' he said (which was).

'Oh-oh!' his aunt said yet again, '*very posh* . . . We shall have to be careful with him then – shan't we? Watch our diction – shan't we? – with him.'

There was no need for her to do that, I thought, for she spoke with a splendid voice and in a most marvellous fashion: pronouncing each word precisely and correctly – except for the occasional softening of an end of a word, caused by a tendency she had to allow her lower lip to sag.

'Yes – very nice,' she went on, as her eyes travelled about my person, and as she continued holding my hand; trying to assess me in some way. 'Very *nice*, Brucey,' she added to Chuck, raising her eyebrows. 'I'm glad you've found someone decent. I wish Molly could. She's taken to juggling, you know. That's the latest thing with *her*.' (Molly, I learned later, was her daughter.) 'As if *that* will get her anywhere in the theatah. Do you go to it, young man?' she said to me. 'Does he go to it?' she asked Chuck, ' – to the theatah?'

'Sometimes,' I answered; having been once since arriving in London; and only to a revue at the Lyric, Hammersmith; in which an actress (Hermione Baddeley, I think) had appeared as Mistinguett; and in a somewhat lewd scene, as I remember, with a feather sprouting from her bottom.

'Well, I'm pleased to hear it,' she said, letting go of my hand. 'It's been my life, you know – hasn't it, Brucey? The theatah? Been my life.'

It was as she said this that she swiftly slipped her hand beneath her pillow, and drew out an enormous wad of banknotes. 'Now, you two,' she said, breathing somewhat quickly, 'I want you to have this;' and wetting one finger with her saliva, slipped two ten-pound notes from the wad, and handed one to Chuck and one to myself.

I must say that I felt terribly embarrassed by this; and had to look at Chuck for guidance – who, fortunately, quickly turned to me and nodded; mouthing to his aunt, as soon as he had done this, that she shouldn't be so 'ex-tra-va-gant'... 'Quickly, now,' she muttered, as we took the notes from her ... 'Before *Jack* comes in,' she whispered, with a twinkle in her eye; which I thought she must have had some instinct about, since, no sooner had we thrust the money into our pockets than Jack appeared at the door.

I won't bore you with the various details concerning the procedures of that day: the lunch with Jack and Bridget in the kitchen; and who, because they looked so alike, I mistook for brother and sister: the walk along the beach, in the bitter cold of the afternoon, in order to get some colour into my cheeks: the curious tea we had, with hard-boiled eggs and things, after the aunt had been half carried to the car, and we had all gone for a brief drive: the countless cups of Bovril that were prepared throughout the day, and that Chuck's aunt Dodo seemed to call for on the hour. Instead, let me carry you forward to about ten-thirty that evening – or night, rather; when Chuck and I, having made our excuses to Jack, who had been plying us with beer, retreated to our room; and I, having been given the priority of the bathroom, where Chuck was now doing his ablutions, was already sitting in bed, reflecting upon the day; and with my half-read detective novel lying open upon my knees.

Chuck came in from the bathroom, carrying his shirt and trousers over one arm, and with only a bathtowel wrapped around his middle. 'Pretty nippy,' he said, as he crossed to throw his clothes on to the bed; then added, 'Better lock the door, I think. We don't want to have Jack marching in in the morning.'

Instinctively (for I was a tidy sort), as Chuck returned to

the door, I quickly stretched out my hands, and started to fold his trousers.

'Oh, thanks, Bo,' Chuck said, reducing my nickname by one syllable, and after he had carefully turned the key. 'Thanks, Bobo,' he repeated; and then, without further ado, released the towel from around his waist, slipped it diagonally across his shoulders; and began rubbing himself with vigour.

He was standing so close to me that it was impossible for me not to look at him at that moment, and to be impressed by the sheer grandeur of his physique; and to see as well, I am afraid, that whoever it was that had fashioned him, had indulged in some monstrous kind of fantasy, by making him so excessively well endowed. 'Chuck,' I said, wanting to divert myself from this encounter, 'why don't you dry yourself by the fire?' as I nodded towards a far corner of the room where an electric fire had been placed, and which was giving the room a glow.

Chuck looked at me; then looked at the fire; then pointed at his forehead with one finger. 'Stupid,' he said – 'You know that, Bo . . .? That's what I am'; and with that remark, and with a short burst of his bouncy giggles, he padded quickly across to the fire; before which he swiftly knelt; and then, once he had draped the bathtowel across his shoulders, he immediately fell silent.

How curiously peaceful it was just then; with the faint sound of the sea beyond the window; and within the room, the occasional ticking-noise of the fire. 'Don't you want your pyjamas, Chuck?' I asked, and then repeated; and said yet again when he failed to answer.

I don't know why I felt so concerned for him at that moment. Was it, perhaps, I thought to myself, because he seemed so oddly like some animal; or that he seemed to be in some way extremely old; as if he might have stepped into the present out of the past?

'Chuck!' I called out, now growing anxious for him, as I scuttled out of the bed, and as I tore his pyjamas from under his pillow . . . 'You'll catch *cold*!' I said . . . 'Here – put them on,' I said, as I rapidly crossed towards him. 'Chuck – *please*. Your pyjamas. *Please*, Chuck – put them on,' I repeated.

Chuck turned to look at me with a deep sadness in his eyes. 'I've got a big one, Bobo – haven't I?' he said to me. 'I've known it since I was twelve . . . and what do you do, Bobo,' he asked, 'with a thing like that?'

'Put on your pyjamas, Chuck – will you?' I pleaded, as he stood up. 'You'll catch pneu*mon*ia, if you go on like that.'

Chuck smiled at me sweetly, took the pyjamas from my hand; then suddenly blurted out; with yet another spurt of his bouncy giggles – 'Well, you might as well be happy with it, as the policeman said to the bishop . . . Isn't that so, Bobo,' he said (he had now slipped on the jacket and was stepping into the trousers) . . . 'Switch off that fire,' he suddenly ordered, 'and back to bed . . . Come along now – *quickly*!' he said, in a matronly kind of fashion, and as if my Auntie Zee was returning. 'Into bed – *fast*!' he said, with a kind of shrill in his voice, as he chased me back to my side of the bed, with a quick gust of hearty laughter.

'Now then – lights *out*,' he commanded, as he towered above my pillow. 'You ready, Bobo?' he asked.

'Yes, Chuck,' I answered, now half buried beneath the blankets, and being made happy by this play. Upon which, Chuck strode across to the door (there were no smaller lights at the sides of the bed); switched off the switch, to plunge us into darkness; and then picked his way through the shadows to climb quickly in beside me.

Again, a silence fell between us.

'Goodnight, Chuck,' I ventured, speaking to his back; for he had immediately turned onto his side.

'G'night, Bo,' he answered quietly; then paused; then said with a slight giggle, 'If you want it it's under the bowler.'

'If I *what*, Chuck?' I squeaked back at him, thinking I had perhaps misunderstood his words.

'Oh, it's nothing,' he said, ' – just silliness. You'll learn . . . just get to sleep,' he said, 'there's a good lad; and we'll start again tomorrow.'

And it was in that mood that we finally settled down to sleep; with Chuck's mind, I felt sure, reflecting upon the events of the day; and upon how, as it drew to its close, he had stood before me naked: and with my own beginning to imagine that the feeling I felt right then might perhaps be closer to brotherly love than the feeling I had for George; and that Chuck might possibly have been right, when he gave me the gipsy's warning.


# IV


I FEAR that I may have made that final scene at Bognor too grotesque, and Chuck perhaps too comic. Therefore, what I am feeling a need of doing right now, is upsetting the inkpot over my paper, so that I can give this curious book of mine a patch of blue-black shadow. For when Chuck had knelt before that electric fire, with only a bathtowel over his shoulders, I had seen, when he had turned towards me, how deep the pain was in his eyes; and that on account of – how shall I put it? – the ungainliness of its proportions, he was at times ruled and driven by his body in such a complusive and such an impersonal manner, that he had come to think of it as his cross; and one that he would be forced to carry through life. So that when he had quoted to me – partly in jest, I have to admit – what the policeman had said to the bishop, that 'you might as well be happy with it', he was simply expressing to me his philosphy: which was that it could only be through comedy and humour, and through the skilful appropriation of some bouncy form of cheerfulness, that he would learn not just how to survive, but also how to protect himself against the near-savagery of his condition; which had placed him more with the animals than with the company of men.

And I cannot say, if I am to be truthful, that I hadn't been moved by Chuck at that moment; and that if, as I then described it, I had so quickly asked him to dress himself, and had even said to him, somewhat extravagantly, that he might catch his death from pneumonia, then that in itself was no more than a similar defence against the darkness I had just witnessed; and had served, I suspect – for one needs to be chary about such things – as a similar form of protection against some such darkness in myself.

But even if that *had* been the case; even if, in a way, I had avoided facing Chuck's tragedy – and if perhaps, by doing so, I have made our exchange too comic – that excursion to Bognor Regis had affected me in a very particular way; for it had given me a view of Chuck that was very much different from before; in that he was no longer only my Auntie Zee, or some rather smartly-dressed city gentleman, who occasionally wore leather: he had also become a kind of brother-figure to me, and so had provided me with family roots in which I was sorely lacking: which could mean, I remember imagining, that my life could begin to grow, and that the action of its story might again begin to move forward.

Two days after our return from Bognor Regis, a letter arrived from Scotland. Chuck had found it in the hallway and had placed it upon my bed.

'Bo,' he said, as I came in, 'there's a letter for you. I've put it on your bed . . . I hope it's not from *him*,' he added with a pout. 'Not from that big blond haggis with frostbite.'

By this time I had opened the letter and was reading it. It was indeed from George; and said –

Dear Richard,

I expect you will be wondering what has happened to me. I rang you several times last week, but could get no reply. Then, when I did get an answer, I had been using the wrong number. Sorry about that; I must have copied it incorrectly. Anyway, this is to tell you that I am in Scotland for a few days, but shall be returning at the weekend. As I don't have your number, and as you are not yet in the book, perhaps you would ring me at the hostel. Or, if you don't fancy doing that, you could meet me at the station. I arrive on Saturday at six.

With very best wishes, and please remember me to Chuck.

Yours affectionately,
George

'What's he say?' asked Chuck, who had been watching me intensely. 'What's he say, Bo?' he repeated.

'Oh, not much,' I replied, attempting to appear nonchalant. 'Just that he's in Scotland: that he tried to ring us last week – but had the wrong number.'

Chuck looked at me with a severe questioning in his eyes. 'He asks after you, Chuck,' I quickly added. 'Remember me to Chuck, he says.'

Chuck swiftly avoided this. 'When's he coming back?' he asked.

'Back . . .? To London . . .? Oh, he doesn't say,' I replied. Then, turning my lie into a half-truth, I said, 'He's there for a while.'

'Then just as well,' said Chuck, showing relief. 'We don't want to have *him* hanging on to us . . . do we, Bo . . .? What *he* spells is trouble. I know. I've told you . . . *Trouble*, Bo – with a capital *"T"*! Now,' he went on, not wanting to think about George any longer, 'what about supper . . .? you in; or you out?'

'In', I said, my mind hurriedly deciding what I might do about George; whether it would be best to ring him after he had arrived, or to meet him at the station: and if the latter, what station it might be, and whether the time he had given was a correct one.

'Well, if it's in,' said Chuck, 'I'd better get some bread. It'll be one of my soups' (Chuck was good at those) 'and some kind of sandwich: whatever I can get'; with which, he slipped on his jacket, and went downstairs to the grocer's.

That, as I say, was on the Tuesday; just two days after our return from Bognor Regis; and George's return was to be four days later – on the Saturday; which I can remember being a peculiar time for me. First of all, because I had said nothing at all to Chuck about George's return, and yet, in spite of that, had already decided that I would be meeting him at the station: having first discovered at which station it would be, and that the time he had given was exact: and also because, on the day following that – the Wednesday – I happened to be browsing in a bookshop in South Kensington (which was somewhat against my usual habits) and came across, and then bought, a paperback by someone called J.C. Hewitt, or Trewitt ( I haven't kept the book, so I am uncertain of the name) that stirred my intellect in an unusual fashion, causing it to become alert and active, and in a way to which I was unaccustomed.

For you will have gathered, I think, that I wasn't a particularly bright person, in what I sometimes think of as those salad days of mine – when, according to Chuck, I was so green it seemed about everything. And even if I did have a tendency to reflect; and on account of that to think; it wasn't in a very trained or organised way; and explains, I am inclined to believe, the addiction I had to detective novels. For whilst these may have given my intellect a degree of exercise; and in much the same way, perhaps, that such a thing might be said about crossword-puzzles; they certainly didn't stimulate me in any very lively fashion; and partly made me, as I now see (though this is not intended as an extended pun upon the term 'salad days') into something of a cabbage.

Anyway, the book – the one that I purchased in South Kensington, and that I did so on the Wednesday after the Tuesday on which George's letter had arrived, was called *The Mystery of the Virgin*; and was one of a rash of books that were appearing at the time – all of which were questioning religion: books that tried to prove, for example, that Jesus wasn't divine; in the sense, that is, that he was simply a very intelligent individual, who had been blessed with the power of striking, radical thought; and trying to pooh-pooh the idea that he was the Son of God; and things like that.

This one – *The Mystery of the Virgin* – did something similiar with regard to the Virgin Birth; and put forward the idea that Mary had not been impregnated by the Lord, so to speak, but by Joseph, her husband. But she didn't know it – in the sense, I mean, that she wasn't aware that she was pregnant, which one gathers can be the case. And it tried to say as well, that because she, Mary, had had rather a rough ride of it, on her way with Joseph to Bethlehem, where they had come to register for their taxes, the birth had been brought on – prematurely; and which was why, of course, they had to repair to an inn for the night: where, with there being insufficient accommodation (perhaps because a lot of other Josephs and Marys were in town with the same idea – of registering for their taxes, that is) they had been obliged to make do with a stable.

Then, it said, when the birth finally occurred, people began to speak of it as a magical child, and one that by some means or another had bypassed the normal process of conception; and that there was no more to the story than that. It was all a question of ignorance and misunderstanding – and of amazement too, of course; which, no doubt, such a thing might induce in anyone.

I won't go into it in more detail. It was one of those argumentative pieces of writing, trying to explain things away: trying to be what is called logical and sensible, and trying to make religious concepts seem improbable. But it set my mind ticking over – and, as I have already said, in a way that was unfamiliar to me: so that if I think of it in that fashion, one could say, I suppose, that it is really on account of that book that my mind began to develop; and perhaps too – who knows? – is what might be partly responsible for the writing of this book.

For it occurred to me then, that what was so missing from that book about the Virgin – and, indeed, as much from the life around me at that time, as it seems to be missing from the life around me today – was a respect for the mystery of any kind of myth; and because of that, a true respect for the human mind; which, as I saw it then (and, indeed, as I still see it now) is bound to rely at times upon symbols that it cannot possibly comprehend; simply because there is – *has* to be – so much ignorance in the world, that we cannot hope or expect to know all; and that what is surely required of us, in the face of such a fact, is some kind of modesty and humility.

I can remember clearly how my mind began to race forward at that moment: how it began so rapidly to put two and two together; telling itself that even if the book I bought *had* seemed to make sense; and even if the argument it put forward *did* seem to be in some way persuasive; what it totally failed to see was that what the collective mind was in need of, at that moment when Christ was born in Judea, was some new sign – or symbol, rather – upon which it could project; and that there was nothing wrong with that. It carried the meaning for which it had been seeking – that was the important thing; and because of that, was able to establish a new truth; which, in this case, obviously had something to do with bringing the godhead down from the skies and placing it here, inside us, upon earth.

However, all that guff – that jaw, is just to show how things were changing for me at that time. So enough of that, and on with our story; which now, as you can imagine, must move swiftly on to that Saturday when George was due to arrive, and when I had planned to meet him at the station.

Not often, perhaps, but occasionally, one can fairly say, I think, that luck is on one's side; and it certainly seemed to be on my side right then; for just as I was worrying myself sick about what I might say to Chuck – what excuses I might make, to ensure that I would be free; and when I had begun to concoct various wild-brained stories in my mind, such as that I had met someone at work, who had asked me to go to a football match at Stamford Bridge; or to go ice-skating (both of which would avoid Chuck wanting to accompany me, because they were activities he disliked); he suddenly announced, out of the blue, that he himself would be out all day – with Darby. Where, he didn't say; and I, of course, didn't ask; partly because I never sought to pry into his affairs, and also, of course, because I was so delighted.

'And I'll be late,' he had said, '– about elevenish . . . You don't mind, do you, Bobo?' he had added, and which you can understand that I didn't.

'I'll probably go to a film,' I replied brazenly. 'There's a good one on at The Curzon. It's about a man who steals a bicycle.'

'About a *what*?' asked Chuck.

'About a bicycle: someone steals one. It's Italian.'

'Oh – one of *those*,' sneered Chuck, who had a fear of all things foreign. 'Why you should want to go to those things, Bobo, I can't think. They're all made by commies; by a bunch of bloody reds. You know that – don't you?'

For once my tongue slipped, and I answered back. 'And what's wrong with that?' I said: not sourly, but with a hint of aggression in my voice.

Chuck looked at me with eyes that seemed made of glass. 'What's *that* you say?' he demanded sharply. 'Do I hear rightly – or do I not?'

He seemed to be daring me to repeat myself; so in the spirit of Cain responding to Abel (or perhaps it was the other way around) I spoke up for myself again.

'I said,' I said, 'what's wrong with *that*?'

It was obvious from Chuck's expression that he was astonished by my reply. 'Have you ever met any?' he asked, in a falsely cool and collected manner, but which I could hear was deeply aggressive.

'Well, *have* you, or *haven't* you?' he insisted.

'No,' I said.

'Well, that just shows – doesn't it? – that you don't know what you are talking about.'

'Have *you*?' I threw back at him, unable to let go.

'Yes,' he said flatly, as if certain that this would finish it.

'Where?' I asked.

'Where?' he almost shouted at me: '*Where*?'

'Yes, where? Where have you met any?'

'*Every*where! That's where I've met them. Ev-er-y-where! So I'm warning you: that's what I'm doing. Don't get too clever, Bobo. Just watch it. Don't start joining *that* mob – will you?'

Unfortunately, I still couldn't let the matter drop.

'There are a lot of poor people in Italy,' I said, 'as there are here: so someone's got to speak up for them. You don't know about that, Chuck – do you? About being poor?'

This time, Chuck stared at me with eyes that seemed made of steel, more than of glass.

'And neither do *you*,' he snorted.

'Oh, yes I do,' I went on again. 'I was brought up in a home, Chuck – you're forgetting that. I never had anything. Any parents, any money – nothing!'

Chuck's lips curled viciously at this remark. 'Poor little *thing*,' he said. 'Poor Bobo. You were just a little orphan – weren't you? Had no mummy or daddy . . . Shit on you! *That's* what I say! Shit on you, Bobo!' – and with that he turned his back on me and stomped out of the room.

By the Saturday, things had calmed down, and Chuck was again his bright, breezy self. He got up early; sang loudly in the bathroom – warbling away, as he shaved and dressed; and as I, wanting to keep clear of him, had lingered on in bed. 'I'm off then,' he had called out, once he was ready. 'If Darby rings, tell him I've left. Say,' he said, looking at his watch, 'that I'll be at his place by nine-fifteen at the latest.'

I made an effort as he said this, and smiled at him in as affectionate a manner as I could muster.

'Bye, Bo,' he said.

'Bye, Chuck,' I answered.

'Remember,' he replied, with one of those bouncy, Auntie-Zee giggles of his, 'if you can't be good, be careful,' spelling out the word 'c a r e f u l' letter by letter.

'Don't worry, Chuck – I'll be good,' I answered him, smiling again; and thinking to myself that I would do my best to be the opposite; and that, as far as 'careful' was concerned, that, today, with Chuck being out until late, and with his being no bother to me in that respect, was a thing that I could forget about.

The day passed: the evening came; and at five I left for the station, arriving there well before six, and wearing what I thought were clothes suitable for the occasion: slacks and a heavy sweater, beneath a short, navy-blue donkey-jacket, that was in fashion in those days. And the train was on time: on the very dot of it – which I thought to myself with a smile it was bound to be, if it was George's train. Nothing with him would not be on schedule. All, I felt sure, would be as he said; and would always be like that. That was the type of confidence I seemed to have placed in him: that he would always be fair, reasonable and exact; and that there would never be 'scenes', as there had begun to be with Chuck. If I got to know him better, I thought, he wouldn't pick on me; wouldn't attempt, as Chuck did, to put me down, or to make me feel small; but would give me room and encouragement; and help me to grow – which was a thing I was needing so much to do just then. Already, as I waited upon the station platform, I was convinced that I was at least an inch taller than I had been just a week ago; and that that pointed, pigeon-boned chest of mine had put on at least a pound or so of extra flesh; so that I felt less skinny in build than I had ever done before: and even my hair seemed to be less wispy; and felt as though it had somehow draped itself across my forehead in a more flattering and more attractive manner; so that, all in all, I had quite a decent view of myself by the time the train arrived from Scotland, and before I saw George – at the far end of the platform, striding towards me with a smile; having first closed the carriage door, which he was bound to do, of course; and having raised one hand to me in salute.

'So you came,' he said, as he clutched my hand. 'You came to meet me, Richard.'

I have no idea what I replied to this. All I can remember is the extreme happiness I felt: the pleasure it gave me to be meeting him in secret, as you might say; and to have been able to guard that secret since the Tuesday.

'How's Chuck?' asked George, as he handed his ticket to the attendant, and I the one that I had bought just for the platform; which was a thing you could do in those days.

'He's out,' I said, 'for the day; and won't be back until eleven': then added, wanting to say this to him quickly – 'He doesn't know about your arriving today. I haven't told him that I am here.'

It was as I said this that we became caught up in a great surge of people leaving the station; and as we were swept up in the crowd, George gripped me firmly by the arm, and guided us along. There seemed to be no question about where we were going. Both of us, without exchanging a word, picked our way across the busy street, now thick with the rush-hour traffic, and made our way to the bus-stop opposite, where a bus seemed almost to be waiting for us, and which bore us quickly off into the night; hurtling its way towards South Kensington, and to the flat that I shared with Chuck; and which now, for that one evening, had become temporarily my own.

'Well, Richard,' said George, once we had taken off our coats, and had switched on the electric fires, and had begun to make the place feel comfortable, 'so you came to the station.'

'Shall I make us some coffee?' I asked nervously, 'or some soup, perhaps? Something to warm us?'

'No,' answered George, authoritatively. 'No soup. Coffee, perhaps, but no soup . . . we're eating out,' he said. 'My old man gave me a hundred; so we can dine in style.'

'A hundred?' I asked, unable to believe my ears.

'Yes,' said George.

'Pounds?' I asked, screwing up my nose.

You must understand that a hundred pounds was a lot of money in those days; and that if you were careful, you could live on it for weeks.

'Yes,' said George, 'he's always doing that: being mean as hell for most of the time – then suddenly doling out something big.'

You may call it unfair of me – unduly secretive, perhaps – but I have no intention of describing the rest of that evening: what type of restaurant we chose; where exactly it was; whether the food was good or bad; what George had said to me about his girl; how happy I felt, and how certain I was that George did too: nor how careful George had been with regard to the time, and how we had left the restaurant at ten o'clock sharp, in order for George to have collected his suitcase from the flat; and to have gone off to the hostel before Chuck had a chance to return. What I want to be clear about is the feeling I had – the near joy I felt, to be free of Chuck for a while; and to know that now at last (and this was for the first time in my life) I had found someone to whom I belonged, and that I could turn to in times of trouble: when, for instance, Chuck might choose to round on me again; and when, as I had already sensed that it must, the brotherly fight between us would break out again, and would become, as I was already imagining, some rather ugly form of power-struggle.

'Thanks for everything,' I said, once George had gathered up his bags and was about to leave, 'for the drinks, the dinner – for everything.'

George looked deeply into my eyes (or at least I thought he did that). 'You don't need to thank *me*, Richard,' he said, with that disarming Clydeside accent of his; 'I'm the one who has to thank *you*.'

'Me!' I exclaimed, genuinely puzzled, since the evening had given me so much pleasure, and hadn't cost me a single penny.

'Yes,' he said, 'you'; and then, sensing that I still didn't quite understand, took hold of me and pulled me close to him.

'Oh, Richard,' he sighed; hugging me, and then patting my back. 'Richard, Richard,' he repeated; and with that, clasped his hands firmly over my ears, and kissed me upon the lips.

Once George had gone, I immediately became anxious that he might have left some trace of his presence; his gloves, perhaps – or even his handkerchief; imagining, as I did, that Chuck might know, by some kind of instinct, that George had been there; and that if he had proof of it, all hell would break loose. So I scoured the place thoroughly to make sure. And then, once I was, I quickly turned down the covers of my bed; undressed; put on my pyjamas; switched off all the lights (except for the one in the small entrance-hall) and pretended to settle down for the night: knowing full well that I wouldn't sleep, and that nothing in the world would allow me to do so until I was sure that the danger had passed, and that my secret was safe; and that, having now guarded it for almost a week, I could choose a time that would be my own to break the news of George's return.

But it wasn't until after eleven-thirty, and perhaps getting on for twelve, that I heard the key turn in the door, and saw, through my half-closed eyes, that Chuck had come in; and was checking to see that I was in my room.

'You asleep, Bo?' he whispered.

I pretended to stir, thinking to myself that it might be wise to make him believe that he had just awakened me.

'Bo,' he whispered again – 'you asleep?'

Quite honestly, there was such tenderness in his voice that I couldn't help mumbling to him that I was not.

'Have a nice evening?' he asked.

'Mmm,' I murmured.

'Good. I'm pleased,' he said.

'– night, Chuck,' I then muttered, thrusting my head into my pillow, to indicate that I really wasn't fully awake, and that I had no wish to chat with him more.

'Goodnight, Bo,' he whispered back at me, in the most delicate tones imaginable. 'See you in the morning,' he said; then closed the door quietly and went out.

The day after that – the Sunday – was one of what Chuck and I used to speak of as our 'stewy' days – though perhaps 'steamy' days would have been a more appropriate way of describing them; when we would do our washing, for instance, or Chuck would make more of his soup; or when we would both have baths, and press our trousers, and make ourselves generally ready for the week ahead. It was a day that I always enjoyed; partly, I suppose, because there was such a lack of domesticity in my background; and partly as well because it was on these days that Chuck seemed at his best. Busyness was what he needed: to be getting away from himself, and from that ill-proportioned body of his: so that on these 'stewy' days, as we used to refer to them, he would be as happy as a lark; singing excerpts from Gilbert and Sullivan, which I detested; or sometimes a snatch or two from some currently popular song or melody (just then, it would have been songs from *Oklahoma*, I suspect, and words like 'the grass is as high as an elephant's eye', which I remember appealed to Chuck enormously) – and it would go on like that all day, with us going in and out of our bedrooms, our bathroom and our kitchen, and not wanting to leave the flat, even for a walk, or to go to the cinema.

And on that particular day – that Sunday – I remember how everything – that whole 'stewy' business of ours, was heightened by the knowledge I had that, rather than being on the bonnie banks of the Clyde, where I knew that Chuck in his mind assumed him to be, George was no more than a matter of yards away; and by the knowledge I had too that, if I really felt the need of it, I could ring him at the hostel; could – if I made some excuse (such as to get a newspaper, perhaps) – simply run downstairs to the street and use the phone box on the corner.

But there was no need for me to do that; because George and I had agreed not to meet that day; and that he would ring me at work on the Monday, so that we could make our arrangements then. Which meant that the day proceeded as normal, until eventually, once all the chores had been done, and once all the bathing and pressing was finished, Chuck and I moved ourselves into the kitchen and settled down to our supper.

I really don't know what put the words into my head, but no sooner had Chuck served us one of his soups, and I had cut and handed him some bread – a huge chunk of it, as he liked it – than I said to him:

'You know Bridget, Chuck; who works for your aunt at Bognor?'

'Bridget?' he answered vaguely, showing that he had no idea of what I was talking about.

'Yes: at Bognor; who does the cooking.'

'Well, of course I do,' said Chuck rather sharply, now wondering why I was asking this.

'Is she Jack's sister?' I asked.

'Is she *what*?' Chuck replied, now showing some interest.

'Is she his sister? Jack's. Are they brother and sister?'

'No: *of course* not,' he answered abruptly. 'What a stupid thing to say . . . they're lovers.'

'Lovers!' I exclaimed.

'Yes,' said Chuck, 'they're always at it. That's why Dodo won't have her live in; because of the noise. She wouldn't sleep, she says, in spite of her deafness.'

'But Chuck,' I said, 'Bridget's –'

'– Older than Jack? Yes, she is . . . So what?'

'Well – I just didn't think that they would be *that*; that they would be lovers. And I thought that Jack was – well, you know –'

'Yes. He is. Of course he is. He likes anything – that's the truth about him, the randy old sod. He'd stuff a rabbit, if he got hold of one.'

I couldn't help laughing at that remark, even if it was the type of talk I never liked to encourage in Chuck.

'But they look so *alike*,' I said.

'Who?' – Chuck looked up from his soup spoon – 'Jack and Bridget?'

'Yes. Don't you think so, Chuck? That they're alike?'

Chuck paused; thought about it a little, and then agreed with me. 'I suppose they are,' he said, 'now that you mention it. But they're lovers: that's what they are.' (He had now gone back to enjoying his soup.) 'She can't have enough of it – that's Bridget's trouble. She's like me,' he said.

'She's nice though – isn't she?' I continued, 'I like her. But I can't imagine her without that turban she wears.'

'Can't what?' muttered Chuck, somewhat grumpily, his mind more on his soup than on my words.

'– Imagine Bridget,' I replied, 'without that turban she wears.'

'I suppose not,' said Chuck, now not interested. 'Eat your soup, Bo – for goodness sake! I don't go to the bother of making it, just for you to sit and talk, and let it go cold . . . Get on with it now. Bridget's just a whore. That's what she is, if you have to know. Now: eat your *soup*!'

The mind is such a peculiar thing though – isn't it? I cannot for the life of me think what had make me talk like that about Bridget. I had spent so little time with her and Jack, during that day at Bognor Regis; yet for some reason, I kept seeing her in my mind; registering in my memory the extreme care she took over everything: opening the oven door, for instance, when she was cooking, with what seemed an excessive amount of caution: or touching the cutlery that she had placed upon the table: not once, but several times, patting it lightly: and also, as she waited for the vegetables to boil, I could see clearly in my mind how she had placed one hand upon her hip, when she had turned to smile at Chuck and myself, as we sat waiting at the table. And even now, in spite of Chuck's replies, I still wasn't satisfied, regarding my knowledge of her.

It is quite impossible to explain why, but I remember thinking to myself that if I judged the moment rightly, I could get Chuck to tell me more. How Bridget and Jack had first met, perhaps; or how she – or perhaps both of them – had come to be working for Chuck's aunt. Was it some kind of sense I had about people: some kind of instinct, perhaps, that lay dormant in me; and that on that week of weeks, as I now think of it, was beginning to come alive? Did I – I wondered – have some kind of inner knowledge: some kind of foreknowledge, that someday, at some unknown time in the future, Bridget would mean something more to me, or something other to me, than the lady who cooked for

Chuck's aunt? Or was that just another of my fancy imaginings; another tale I had spun in my mind; and the result, perhaps, of that addiction I had to detective stories?

'Bo!' Chuck shrieked out at me, his mouth half full of bread. 'Will you *please* eat your *soup*!'

'Sorry, Chuck,' I answered, because I really was; and because I really did appreciate the bother he had gone to in making it; and because, after all, he really was so good at it. In fact, if you want to know, of all the soups that I have tasted in my entire life, Chuck's must be counted the best; particularly one that he made with leeks and a few potatoes, that was always rich and creamy, and in which the pieces of vegetables were truly enormous; and which seemed to reflect, now that I think of it, that generous side of his nature that related to his good cheer; and that he used, as I had seen at Bognor, in order to keep himself at a distance from the more tragic side of his being.

# V

IT'S QUITE SOMETHING, I find, to be making myself the subject of a book: to be going into so many details about myself: about my physique, my looks – the colour of my hair and eyes; the shape of my ears; and even speaking of something I am a little self-conscious about, which is that my chest is somewhat pointed in the manner of a bird's; and which made me speak of myself at one point as having been a fledgling unable to fly.

But that's writing, I suppose. It's rather like taking a good full frontal look at yourself in a mirror: something I was never keen on doing in the past, and that I'm still not keen on doing today.

And writing's not easy, I discover. In fact, drawing any of that old blue-black blood out of *me* seems much like drawing that other kind from a stone; just one small penful of it appears to be difficult! Not that I'm lazy, exactly – I can't quite accuse myself of that: but I'm so *slow*. By which I mean that whereas my guess is that the majority of writers will slap down two or three thousand words a day; with me, it'll be a page or so if I'm lucky, and if I'm feeling in the mood. And then, I've got this thing in my mind about throwing nothing away; which means that if I mention someone or something – even a minor character or event, then you can bet your bottom dollar that I'll be using it again.

Brick by brick, is how I think of it; and no wastage either; neither of labour nor of thought; which indicates a tidyish sort of mind, I suppose: though you wouldn't think that when I first jot down an idea, which I do in such awful scribble. Later, though, when I write the stuff out, I do it more decently, and I then have quite a reasonable hand. And once I've done that, I'll go over it with a fine red pen and make my corrections – which I then copy out and paste over, and which means (because I'm so seldom really satisfied with what I think of as the 'sound') I'll mostly rewrite and paste over again – and maybe yet again; so that my manuscript, which is done on a thinnish kind of paper, gets thicker and thicker in patches, until parts of it become as thick as a piece of card.

So I'm something of a fusspot, I suppose; liking to have things orderly. And I suspect I've got a thing about numbers as well. Because do you know what? – I've made a kind of pact with myself that each chapter of this book – in the *ms.*, that is – will be no more than twenty pages long; or, rather, will be almost exactly that in length; so that there will be a kind of regular pattern of reading, that will give the book a structure. Which sounds all right, but of which I daresay I ought to be suspicious. Still, I don't think I should deny myself that – do you? I mean, such quirks of the mind are to be found in everyone: like in the old gentleman who lived across the street from us – meaning from the flat that I shared with Chuck – and who would always cross it at the same point: never at the corner, where it would be safer, but always directly across from us; and which meant that sometimes he'd be forced to wait for ages before there'd be a suitable break in the traffic. It's just one of those things. A kind of fetish of the mind.

But that's all part of the art of it, I guess; all part of the business of being a writer. It's going into the details of things that counts; because by using them, it seems that you can build up a picture of different people and places that gradually makes them seem real. Not real, of course, in the sense that you have copied them from life, but because they – those details – have suddenly sprung to mind; in the way, I mean, that I have just recalled, and for no apparent reason, that old gentleman who lived opposite; and who had that odd habit when crossing the street.

Then, another thing I have to be honest about is the fact that I so resented being an orphan. I don't quite know whether I believe in a God or not, because I've no real proof that one exists; but if he does – or if *she* exists, for that matter – then why was I made to be that, I wonder: to be without parents and so loveless, and without a real name of my own? That's a pretty mean trick to have played, I think. And then to have made me so inhibited too, and so green about things in general. That's not exactly a nice thing to have had done to one either.

Still, I shouldn't complain too much, I suppose, because

there are much worse things that could have happened: and it's not the end of the world – is it? – to be lacking in parents and in love; and to have had, as yet, as friends, only this rather monstrous fellow called Chuck, and this possible friend-to-be, as I sometimes thought of him, who hailed from Bonnie Scotland.

The question now arising in my story, of course, is what George was going to be for me. Friend, soul-mate, companion? Lover perhaps? Who knows? Quite honestly, I didn't mind much *what* he was to be. The main thing was to have just *someone* in my life: someone who really meant something – to me, I mean; because I was sick to the teeth of being so cut off from people, and having no real feeling for anyone – no really *deep* feeling, that is. I just wanted to get involved, so that I could find out who I was.

You might tell me, of course, that I was already involved with Chuck, and I guess you are right about that. And it's true, I daresay, that I had already discovered at least *something* about myself through him, and therefore should have been grateful. But it was difficult for me to be that. I am not sure why. Was it because he was more of a brother to me than a real friend, and a mother at times as well; and because brothers and brothers and sons and mothers don't quite have that type of relationship.

Then another thing, since I am going into such matters. Why was I so coy, I wonder, about that scene at night in the flat, after I had met George at the station; saying that I didn't intend describing it in detail? Surely, that must have seemed a bit of a letdown – on my part, I mean, as a writer. I mean, it's not as if we were teenagers or something. We were both grown men in our twenties, and it must seem unlikely to you that nothing more would have happened. I'm not saying that I ought to have written in some great love scene, or that George and I should have jumped straight into bed together, because I've been trying to edge you towards the idea that George was more confused and more uncertain of himself than I perhaps had been wanting him to be. But at least we'd have had a good talk about ourselves, I think, and about what our feelings were for each other – or, at least, I would like to believe that we would have done that; and wish that I had allowed you to believe it too.

And then, you must have thought it a bit of a cheek of me to have ended that scene with a kiss; unless, of course, you accepted that I was trying to show that George couldn't control himself, and that, after having been recently ditched by his girl, he was clinging to the next thing that presented itself – which was me. That would be correct, I think, because people do do that sort of thing – don't they? Do use others to catch their balance; and sometimes, as far as their actions are concerned, don't quite know why they are behaving compulsively, and why they do the things that they do.

Still, from what you've been told, it is perfectly obvious that George was prepared to make further arrangements, in that he had agreed – or said to me, rather – that he would be ringing me on the Monday: and, moreover, was being as secretive as I was about our relationship: not saying, for instance, that he would either ring me; or would call for me at the flat; but would telephone the estate office where I worked: so he couldn't have been *all* that unconscious of his actions.

Then, another thing I have to clear up. You have been told – told by me, that is – that I had spent some time at a technical college; but what I haven't bothered to let you know is that I had been trained to be a surveyor, and because of that had quite a genuine interest in such things as architecture and building. You may have guessed this, I suppose, by the reference there was to Ruskin at one point; but it wasn't much of a clue. Yet that is what I was – or had been trained to be; and yet, at the same time, it seems that I was doing some kind of clerical work at an estate agent's near Harrods: which isn't exactly the work of a surveyor – is it? So why was that, you might ask? Why didn't I have a proper job? – The type of job for which I was qualified? Was it because I hadn't got down to it as yet; because there was a part of me that was delinquent; and that I was as yet unable to hold down what one might call a decent, professional position? I suppose it could have been that, because I've already made clear to you that I was retarded in some way; by saying, for example, that I was a fledgling unable to fly, and that I saw myself as being only partly formed – both in body and in mind. And it could be that there are more people like that than one cares to think. Even though they may dress in smart, professional suits and things, some men – and some women too, I expect – remain boys and girls underneath; and for longer than one might imagine.

And yet another thing that I want to have a go at myself about, is the fact that I haven't said a single word to you about the efforts I made when I was small. How, in spite of my having been brought up in a 'home', I had been extremely diligent at school, and had done well; passing my exams; winning a scholarship from primary school on to a grammar school, which was one of the finest in the country; and then, winning a further one to that technical college, where I had been trained to be a surveyor. I really think that I could have told you about that; if only to show that, although I may have become blocked and stuck in my ways by the time I came to meet Chuck, I was never really a dunce. And that too is a thing that can happen to people. They can be as bright as buttons when they are small; pass their exams; get themselves forward – on to further schools and colleges: and then, once they are in their twenties, everything gets blocked: some part of themselves, which they have probably neglected, suddenly catches up with them. Perhaps (these are just examples) they hadn't had enough water-play when they were small; or enough sex in their teens; or weren't taught to handle money properly. There are so many things like that; that can become neglected; and then – 'wham' again! – like that mad woman in *Jane Eyre*, it suddenly loosens itself, and breaks free of its cupboard.

In my case, although you may think it was (simply because people put so much down to it these days), I don't think the blockage was connected at all with sex. I really don't. I may not have had very much of it after my late teens and up to the time when I came to meet Chuck, but I had had an awful lot of it when I was younger, and had been cooped up in that 'home'; and the long winter nights had been so boring. Also, at college, later, where everyone seemed to be at it in some form or another. No, it was more, I think, that I needed for a while to be alone; to be on my own; to be free of other people; and that I needed to do this because of my background; because of my lack of personal identity – having no parents and things; and in order perhaps to centre myself.

At least, that could be one of the reasons. Another, as I see it, could be something yet again, and not so easy to speak about; and which, as I have suggested earlier, has nothing to do with cause and effect, but is simply 'my story'; the one that I have to tell – to live out: almost – if we were speaking of music, for example – as if there was some rhythm I had to honour; that because my early years had been so deliberate (in the sense, I mean, that, through my having made such efforts to better myself, they had been so forward-looking and driven) I then needed to do the opposite, which was nothing.

I know you can say that that too sounds like cause and

effect; but it isn't really – or it isn't quite, at least; because if we are thinking in terms of rhythm, then surely the rhythm of our life must begin on the day we are born; which means that our story has more to do with time, perhaps, than with things that have actually happened to us, through our environment: the time at which we have stepped into the world, and the rhythm to which we then become connected as a result.

Anyway, that's my idea, and I think I would have given myself some credit if I had spoken up for myself in that way. At least people (meaning, you, the reader) might have had a better impression of me; and perhaps it would have helped to make more sense of the projection I had upon George: that my time of pause was coming to an end; and that what I was doing was seeking some kind of 'George' figure in myself, that would connect me with life's action again, and would free me from the stagnation from which I had been suffering.

Now; having had that real 'beef' about myself, and having cleared up a number of things that had been bothering me; and that I somehow feared had perhaps been bothering you; I must let my thoughts fade into the background again, and must return once more to the main narrative of this book, and to what George said to me on the telephone, when he rang me at the office: which was on the Monday following that 'stewy' Sunday in the flat, when Chuck and I hadn't gone out; and when I had asked him those odd questions about Bridget.

'Can I speak to Richard Constable, please?' There! Now you know my surname at last: not a real one exactly, but the one that I had been given; and not after the great East Anglican painter, as I would have hoped, but after the burly policeman ('constable' – get it?) who had found me upon his doorstep.

'George, it's me – Richard,' I said; having answered the phone myself, and having recognised his voice immediately.

'Oh, Richard. Good. How are things? How was it yesterday?'

'Fine,' I said. 'Chuck was at his best: no scenes; no tempers.'

'Did you tell him?' George asked.

'What? – that you are back?'

'Yes. Did you say anything?'

'No, but I'm going to. I don't know when. Tomorrow, perhaps.'

'And what about tonight; about this evening? I was wondering if we could meet?'

'Oh, yes – we can,' I said, having prepared myself for this. 'I told Chuck I'd probably be late. And I don't have to tell him what I'm doing – do I? I'll just say that I stayed on late at work; and then went for a drink, perhaps.'

'You sure?' asked George, sounding anxious.

'Yes, of course I am,' I asserted. 'He doesn't tell me where *he's* going, or what *he's* doing, so what's there to stop me from doing the same?'

'Nothing, I suppose,' George answered with a laugh. 'You know him better than I do. Anyway, what shall we do? Where shall we meet? Do you want me to come to the office? I shall be free just before five.'

I hesitated, not being certain about the office, though I don't know why; but then thought better of it.

'Yes,' I said, 'that would be fine. We could go to a film, perhaps. There's a good one on at The Curzon.'

The idea of us going to the cinema seemed clever of me, I thought; because as yet, Chuck hadn't questioned me about the Saturday, and about whether I'd been to the Italian film or not; and I thought that if George and I had seen it – or if *I* had, rather – then I would have something that I could use, if I should choose to guard my secret for longer.

So that is what we did. George met me shortly after five, when I had just finished work, and off we went to an early show at The Curzon; which we both enjoyed enormously: not only (or even as much) because of the political slant of the film, but because it was such a deeply human story, and done in such an effective manner, and seemed so truthful, as a result: so that when we left the cinema we felt elated; enjoying that form of spiritual lift that a work of art can provide, and feeling better and cleaner for it; as though our souls had been given a good bath; and not so much for ethical reasons (though in a film of that kind, which concerned the poor, that was bound to be part of its effect) but because the work was so wrought, and seemed in some way to be so enchanted: somewhat in the way, perhaps, that an early Italian painting can be that.

'Truly excellent,' said George, when we had found a restaurant where we could eat, and that I had insisted should be a cheap one. 'Excellent,' he repeated – meaning the film, of course, and which it really had been . . . But then, once we had ordered our food, and once we had decided upon beer rather than wine, we began to talk about ourselves; and to say some of the things I had hoped we would say on the Saturday, but which apparently, we didn't.

'You know, Richard,' said George. 'I am terribly sorry about the other night.'

'Sorry?' I answered. 'Why?'

'Because I am. Because I got you plastered – didn't I? Because I don't think you'd have drunk as much on your own.'

I felt relieved, because I had thought at first that he was speaking of that second evening we had spent together, after I had met him at the station.

'Well, what if you did?' I replied. 'That's what I needed to do – to let go. I enjoyed it . . . Even if it put Chuck's back up, it was still worth it, I think . . . And in any case, Chuck doesn't concern me. I just share the flat with him; and that's all . . . So why should he?'

'He's very fond of you,' said George, rather pointedly. 'You do know that – don't you, Richard?'

'Well, maybe he is,' I answered. 'So I'm fond of him too; in a way. But it's not as if we were – you know – together.'

It was as I said this that I noticed that George's eyes had gone blank, and imagined that he either hadn't registered what I had said, or that he was quickly blotting it from his mind.

'You do understand that – don't you, George?' I repeated, 'that Chuck and I aren't together.'

'Oh, well,' said George, as his eyes came back into focus, 'you are in a way, you know. Perhaps you aren't aware of it, Richard, but you are in a way.'

'And that bothers you?' I asked.

'Oh, no – no,' said George, shaping his mouth as though he was about to whistle. 'No,' he repeated, 'but I think you should know; should realise – that's all. Things like that are strong. Take me and my girl, for instance; we were together for *years*, Richard; ever since we were at school; and you can't break easily from such things.'

'But I've known Chuck for only a few weeks!' I protested. 'Years may be different – but *weeks*?'

'People get stuck to each other,' George said, persisting. 'It's not just the length of time they're together, it's something else. It's been a real blow to me, having my girl walk out on me like that . . . male pride, I suppose; and she's given no real reason for it.'

I felt like saying that there seemed to be plenty of reason for it to me, in that George seemed such an ambivalent figure: but I didn't, because it suddenly occurred to me that she – his girl – may have been equally so; and that, in that respect, they might possibly have been a pair: so I simply said –

'You do seem cut up about it, George. I'm sorry – I really am. I've never had a girl. Never had anyone . . . In fact' (I looked at him carefully when I said this) 'you're the first person in my life that I've felt I could care about. I hope you don't mind my saying that.'

It had taken an enormous effort for me to push my remarks that far; but something in me had been pressing me to do so: forcing me to test myself; to try to know myself better, by judging how I stood in relation to George. The result, however, was quite the opposite of what I was hoping for; in that, instead of breaking through to something, and of opening things up, it merely provoked a rather ugly silence between us that we both found difficult to break – until, that is, I suddenly had the idea that I should speak more to George about his girl.

'Did you see her?' I asked, ' – your girl? When you were in Scotland?'

George had obviously been caught out by this, and looked at me suspiciously; but then, once he had assured himself that I wasn't teasing him, and that, rather than sit silent, I was prepared to talk about anything – even his girl – he relaxed; taking out his pipe, which he seldom smoked, and tapping it cautiously against the table-leg; then packing it with tobacco; then lighting it; and then looking across at me over the flame.

'Yes,' he said, letting out a great puff of smoke, 'just once: briefly. She lives with her parents; not far from my own: in the same street, in fact.'

'And she's nice?' I asked, not because I was curious, but to have something to say.

'She is,' he replied, making that odd whistling shape with his mouth again, ' – very. You'd like her.'

'And have you – slept with her?' I asked, risking another dare.

George paused before answering this, taking a further suck at his pipe. 'Oh, yes,' he said, 'of course . . . Not often, because of us living at home – with our parents; but occasionally, yes. I have. Of course.'

And that was the type of conversation that continued; so that by the time the evening came to an end, my feelings for George had changed; not because he had been sly or evasive – he hadn't. In fact, now that I think about it, he had replied to my various questions in a more direct manner than I had perhaps expected him to do; but as we made our way home on the bus, towards South Kensington, I had the idea that I was being used in some way: that I was merely serving as some kind of bridging-figure for George; carrying him on from one phase of his life to another – and I felt sore about this. It didn't occur to me, of course, that I might be doing the same. That is the difficulty with projection. You aren't aware – or aren't sufficiently – that what you are expecting the other person to be is simply some projected part of yourself; and that, in a sense, what the projection creates is false; so that the view – the picture that it has created – becomes a mirage: something which, by its very nature, must eventually disappear.

And it does create the most complicated feelings. I remember, for instance, how angry I felt inside myself that evening; how drawn I was to pick some kind of quarrel with George, so that I could destroy the power his image had over me. And perhaps I would have done just that – not on the bus, perhaps, but once we were on our own again, in the street, and once we were approaching that corner near our pub, where, as you will recall, our relationship had begun (and where now, this evening we would part; with George going off to his hostel, and I to the flat I shared with Chuck).

But what prevented me from doing this was the fact that, from a distance, I had spotted Chuck; with his friend, Darby: the latter sitting astride an enormous motorbike; and with Chuck standing close to him on the kerb.

Reacting quickly, I touched George lightly on the arm. 'George! – there's Chuck,' I said, as he responded instinctively to my warning. 'He's with Darby.'

George glanced quickly along the street, and in the direction towards which I had nodded. 'He hasn't seen us,' he said, with that firmness and self-assurance he seemed so quickly able to summon. 'He's too busy talking . . . I'll go back,' he said. 'I'll take the next turning: go home the other way.' Then he turned to me. 'Look, Richard,' he said. 'I'll ring you. Not tomorrow, but the day after. We've got a lot to talk about . . . Now,' he went on, 'you will be careful – won't you? – about Chuck. You'd better speak to him: you'd better tell him that I am back: say that you bumped into me or something.'

'I suppose I must,' I muttered, not being keen on the idea.

'So I'll ring you then,' he said, pressing my arm (or perhaps squeezing it would be a better way of describing it) – and with that, turned sharply upon his heels and went off into the night.

It was such a peculiar feeling I had, standing there in the street, as if I had become attached in some way to its shadows; and feeling that I was loitering about suspiciously until Darby steamed away on his bike. For I had not behaved like that in my life, or didn't think that I had. Except, of course, for when I had lied about George's letter. But I didn't feel badly about it, because it had been something I had felt a real need to do; and that, if I had been reluctant to speak to Chuck about George's return, it was because my not doing so had meant such a lot to me; and because I was gaining so much pleasure from that curious moment of shade.

At the same time, however, George's influence upon me was strong; and as I climbed the stairs to the flat, I already knew that I would be doing what he had asked; and that either that evening, within the next hour (or, at the very latest, the next morning over breakfast) I would be speaking to Chuck about George, and bringing the time of my secret to an end.

'Is that you, Richard?' Chuck called out as I came in.

I answered that it was.

'I'm having a crap,' he said, as I went into my room, noticing as I did so that there were two letters on my bed; one of which I could see was a bill; and the other (because I had quickly recognised the handwriting) I could see was from the master of that 'home' where I had been brought up; and which I guessed must be one of the notes he sent me from time to time, saying that if I ever cared to 'come down', as he always put it, he and his wife would be pleased to see me; and which, although I never did do that – go to visit them, I mean – I always answered: not immediately, but within a month perhaps of receiving the letter; and through which an exchange between my present life, and the one that lay behind me in the past – and for which, if I am to be honest, I have little warm or pleasurable feeling – was kept alive.

'You eaten?' asked Chuck, in what I noted was a distinctly gruff tone of voice; and as he came into my room, slipping his braces on to his shoulders.

'Yes,' I answered, placing the letter that I had been handling unopened in a drawer.

'Well, *I* haven't,' said Chuck. 'I've just come in. I'll have some soup.'

'And I'll have a coffee,' I added, seeking a brief moment of pause, before making the announcement I knew that I was about to make. 'I'll get it myself,' I said. 'I'll join you in a minute. Then, once I had removed my tie and jacket and been to the bathroom, and had checked to see that the bill was indeed a bill, and was only for the gas, which was mercifully small, and which I had agreed to pay, I went into the kitchen where Chuck was having his supper.

'Do you know what?' I blurted out, as I was making my coffee. 'Do you know who I bumped into: today – in the street? This evening, in fact?'

'George,' replied Chuck, sipping his soup.

His voice was so quiet and so withdrawn, it threw me out.

'Ye-s,' I said, my voice quaking a little. 'Yes – you're right, Chuck. How did you guess?'

'He's been here since Saturday – hasn't he?' Chuck answered darkly. 'I read his letter.'

'You *what*?' I half shrieked at him, unable to believe my ears.

'I read his letter,' repeated Chuck, in that very flat, emotionless voice that he would use from time to time. 'This morning I did,' he went on, 'after you'd gone out. It was half open by your bed . . . If you don't want me to read your letters, Richard, don't leave them lying about.'

I simply couldn't believe that he was saying this. 'You mean,' I said, 'You read *my* letter? You read one that was addressed to *me*: to me personally?'

'Yes,' answered Chuck, his voice void of all feeling. And then, because I couldn't stop myself, I let rip; turning swiftly from the draining-board and throwing my coffee cup across at him; hitting the table, and spilling its contents over the bread and onto the butter; into the salt and into the soup.

'You *bastard*, you!' I screamed. 'You bastard, Chuck! . . . You know damned well that you've no *right* to do that! You've no right to read my letters!'

Chuck said nothing. Instead, he simply rose from his seat and brought my cup across to the draining-board; then took up the dishcloth, and used it to wipe and tidy the table.

'You shouldn't lie to me, Richard,' he said, in the coolest tone imaginable. 'I knew something was up, so I read it: this morning; after you'd gone to work. I suppose you saw him on Saturday; and I suppose you've seen him again tonight.'

'Yes – I *have*!' I yelled at him . . . 'So what business is it of yours?'

'Oh, it's none,' he answered, now turning to face me. 'It's no business of *mine*.' Then, as he continued putting things in order; and as he served himself with a fresh plateful of soup, and which I remember to this day was a thick, brownish one he made from lentils; he said, 'Except that you had *agreed*, Richard, *not* to see him; and that you've not kept your word – have you? – that's all.'

It is impossible for me to describe the peculiar coldness of his expression, and the impression he gave of having retreated to some remote area of the mind, from which to pronounce his icy judgement. There was no sign in him then of my Auntie Zee; nor of that new brother-figure of mine, that I had first encountered at Bognor Regis – and where now, suddenly flashing into my mind, I saw the dancing eyes of Jack, as we drove along in the car; and the neat twist of Bridget's hip, as she stood poised beside the vegetables. But what I *did* see; what I *did* recognise, in this icy, cold aloofness of his, were the lofty, disdainful expressions of that 'madam' who ran the hostel, whenever she had summoned me into her parlour; and knew then that there must be points in the human psyche where male and female meet; and where such feelings as love or concern – or, indeed, of pity – are suppressed in the name of righteousness.

And the effect of this (which I sensed must be a part of Chuck's dark cunning) was to make a kind of attack upon the truth; for I found myself dazed and confused, wondering whether I really *had* left the letter by my bed, instead of hiding it carefully in a drawer, where I would have known my secret would be safer. Yet, on account of that distant, icy expression of his, Chuck had somehow convinced me that I had. And this in spite of the fact that within me, lodged somewhere inside myself, and in a much deeper area of the mind, there lay a real certainty of knowledge that the opposite must be true; and that I had indeed placed the letter in a drawer; and that Chuck, in order to read it, must have taken it out and opened it.

So I withdrew from Chuck into silence; allowing him to believe that this was a round he had won; and wondering to myself how long it might be before further troubles would break out, and whether the tension growing between us might be dangerous.

## VI

THE FOLLOWING MORNING I felt dreadful. Chuck and I had said nothing to each other before going to bed; not even a gruff goodnight; and I had slept badly, twisting and turning, and dreaming of a tough, hairy old spider that came spinning down from the ceiling. So I had risen early, hoping to escape from the flat before Chuck was up and about.

It wasn't to be though, because as I was giving myself breakfast in the kitchen, with the gas oven on – and with its door half open to take the chill off the room – he came stumbling in in his pyjamas.

'Sleep well?' he muttered, without looking at me, and as

he drew a glass of water from the tap; and as he then quickly took a gulp from it.

'No,' I answered bluntly, with as little emotion as I could manage.

'No?' he said, pretending to be surprised, and turning his great bleary face towards me. 'Poor little Bobo . . . Now why was that? . . . Why did Bobo have a bad night? . . . Is Bobo sick or something? . . . Shall his Auntie Zee take his temperature?'

'I'm all right, Chuck,' I answered, feeling like kicking him. 'I just didn't sleep too well – that's all.'

As I was saying this, I began carrying my cup and plate to the draining-board; and in order to do this, was forced to pass in front of Chuck, whose sleepy animal eyes followed my movement suspiciously.

'And I'm going out early,' I added. 'I need a good walk.'

'A walk!' said Chuck, glowering at me, and then looking towards the frosted panes of the window. 'In *this* weather!'

'It's not *that* cold,' I answered, heading for the door. 'I'm walking up to the park – and then along by the edge of the Serpentine. I'll go to work that way.'

Chuck followed me into my room. 'You want your head seeing to,' he muttered. 'You're mad, Bo – that's what's wrong with you . . . Going for a *walk*: in the *park*: at this time of the bloody morning.'

'Perhaps,' I answered, 'but it's what I'm going to do'; and taking a long, thick scarf out of my cupboard, I wrapped it carefully around my shoulders before slipping on my donkey-jacket. 'Bye, Chuck,' I said, pushing past him towards our small entrance-hall.

It was obvious that Chuck couldn't believe what he was hearing, and that I should be asserting myself in this way; because he came quickly stumbling after me; and – before I could reach the door to go out, had grabbed me by the arm.

'Now look here, Bo,' he said. 'We're not having more of this hanky-panky – are we? Just because I took a look at George's letter.'

'*Just*,' I said to him with a sneer.

'Yes – just. I was only thinking of you, Bo. As I told you last night, it's no business of *mine* – except that I know his type; and I don't want you to get hurt.'

'I can look after myself,' I said, not wanting to engage with him, and wrenching my arm free from his bearlike grip. 'I'm off,' I said, making for the door. 'I'll see you this evening – if you're in, that is. I'll be home early.'

As I said this, I noticed that Chuck had suddenly relaxed – probably, I thought, because my coming home early that evening meant that I had made no arrangement with George . . . 'Yes,' he called after me, '*I'll* be here . . . Bye, Bo,' he said, as I went down the stairs, and as his voice began to recover its usual, protective cheerfulness . . . 'See you tonight!' he called out; ' – and Bo,' he added, as I reached the turn of the first landing, ' – watch out for your willie in the park. Don't let it get frostbitten – will you?' with which he let out a great fit of his bubbly giggles; and as he twiddled his chunky fingers at me in farewell, retreated into the flat and closed the door.

It was much colder out than I had expected it to be, with a hard film of frost coating the city's rooftops; but the air was relatively clear and pure before much traffic was about; and I was able to enjoy my walk up to the park, then entering it by Prince's Gate, and cutting in to walk by the Serpentine: the size of which is always a surprise to me, whether I encounter it in winter or in summer; or in those lovely spring and autumn days when everything looks at its best; either sparkling with greens and with whites, as it is at the beginning of the year, and with sharp, startling patches of yellow when the daffodils are in bloom; or thick with those heavy ambers of the autumn, when the squirrels are stacking away their nuts; patting the disturbed earth back into place again, once they have buried their secret treasure.

And on that frosty morning in February, it seemed for some reason to be in more of an in-between state; with the trees still dark and bare, and their reflections in the water great patches of moodless shadow; shooting swiftly out from the banks, in the low early light of the morning; then just seeming to hold themselves there; only breaking and trembling a little as an occasional silent ripple of water moved slowly over the surface.

There were few people about: only two, in fact. One, a heavy middle-aged woman, wrapped in what seemed to be a thousand coats and cardigans; and wearing a pair of dirty, yellow-coloured wellingtons, as if she herself might be a goose; and who was tearing savagely at an enormous loaf of bread, as she stooped to feed the various waterfowl that came clucking and quacking towards her; stepping arrogantly out of the water, with their pink webbed feet flapping upon the gravel. And the other, a very sad old man, who might have been a tramp, and who seemed to be bearing upon his shoulders all his worldly possessions; and who looked at me charily as I passed, from beneath bushy, iron-grey eyebrows.

So it refreshed me, and gave me the space that I was needing; and allowed me to recover at least some of my temper and balance by the time I reached the office: although I have to admit, that I still hadn't come to terms with the fact that Chuck had opened my letter; and I found myself wondering, as I turned out of the park, and as I made my way towards Knightsbridge, whether I should forget about it or not.

If Chuck had just said to me that he was sorry, then I knew that I would have quickly buried the hatchet; but what irked me so much was the fact that he had avoided doing that. As yet, unfortunately, I was too unfamiliar with his type; and hadn't understood how, in this respect, he was like a certain kind of expansive, extrovert woman; who, if they make a blunder, in the way that Chuck had made one with me, can never bring themselves to apologise; and will resort to all kinds of twists and turns of the mind in order to avoid such self-confrontation.

But I knew that the day ahead of me was long, and that I had made no plans at all to see George, or even to speak to him on the telephone; and guessed somehow that by the time the evening had arrived, and Chuck and I had both returned to the flat, I would have found a way of coping with last night's upset.

And in any case, I had no desire to pick a real fight with Chuck. We lived too close to each other for that. I just needed to say the right thing – for myself, I mean. Just a word, maybe, or a short sentence; so that I could sleep soundly again, in the way that I usually did; and so that I could think about George rather than about Chuck, whose interest concerned me more.

It took me all day to sort myself out, and before I was able to decide that probably the best thing for me to do was to treat Chuck to a dose of his own rough medicine. So that evening, when I came in, and because I had already heard that Chuck was at home, and had installed himself in the kitchen, I made up my mind that I would be as bright and as breezy in my own way as Chuck could be in his.

'Hello – ee!' I called out, as I closed the door. 'You there, Chuck? Did you have a good day?'

The battery of kitchen noises ceased, and Chuck appeared at the doorway.

'Did I *what*?' he asked, his eyes all agog, and as if I might have been speaking to him in Spanish.

'Did you have a good *day*?' I repeated, and with what I intended to be a grin.

'Oh,' said Chuck, lowering his eyes a little. 'I did – yes. Did you?'

'*Very*,' I answered, taking off my coat. 'What are you doing? Making something for supper? Something nice?'

Chuck couldn't quite cope with this, and for a moment acted coy.

'I bought some fish,' he said, in a rather muted tone of voice. 'Hake,' he said. 'You like it – don't you?'

'*Love* it!' I replied, not sure whether I did or not: then went on – 'Can I give you a hand, Chuck? Is there something that I can do?'

'Give me a *hand*?' said Chuck, raising his eyebrows, as if he might have been some painted dame in a pantomime, and as he turned back into the kitchen. 'The only thing *you're* good at is peeling the bloody spuds; and I've done that already . . . Go and change, Bo,' he said, his voice lifting slightly. 'Have a bath, if you want to. It'll be good for your piles.'

Piles was not a thing that I suffered from, but, nonetheless, I decided that I would follow Chuck's suggestion, and went into my room to change; finding it neater and tidier than I had expected it to be. After the wretched night I had had, I had pictured that everything there would be in disorder; yet my bed was reasonably tidy, with only a pair of socks lying upon it and a vest: and these I quickly put out of sight, once I had removed my jacket and had hung it in the wardrobe; and after I had put my keys and wallet in the drawer of a small table by my bed. Then, as I was taking off my shirt, I suddenly remembered the letter I had received the day before, and that I hadn't bothered to open: so I quickly checked to see that it was where I had put it – in that same drawer of my cupboard, where I had just placed my keys and wallet – and determined that I would take it with me the next day, and would open it at the office.

And at that very moment – and for no reason that I could think of, I suddenly felt happy – perhaps, I told myself, because Chuck and I seemed to be having a 'stewy' kind of evening, and because it was then, when we were being together in that way, that we were always at our best. I can't say that I exactly sang in my bath, because my voice – my singing one – was rather a poor one; but I warbled away in my fashion, and enjoyed the good soak I was having, after what had been a long and difficult day, and after that restless night I had had, dreaming of a tough, hairy old spider.

'Richard!' Chuck's voice came booming through the half open door of the bathroom.

'Yes?' I answered loudly, in case something was amiss, and to make sure that he would hear.

'You're not playing with your willie – are you?'

'What did you say?' I called back at him, pretending not to have heard.

'I said,' he said, his head suddenly poking itself past the door, 'you're not playing with yourself, I hope. Supper's almost ready. So out with you – quick! sharp! Get a move on!'

I laughed and flicked some of my bathwater at him.

'Now then,' he said, putting on a stern expression. 'Enough of that, young man. You've got ten minutes to dry yourself and dress: so out with you. Get *on* with it!'

Obediently, I climbed out of the bath and rubbed myself dry. Then, with a towel wrapped around my waist, I went across and into my room, in order to dress myself by the fire; with only the small lamp on by my bed; the light of which cast long fingerlike shadows, as I slipped quickly into my clothes.

'I'm ready, Chuck!' I called out, as soon as I was. Then,

still combing my hair, the ends of which were as yet damp and heavy with bathwater, I joined Chuck in the kitchen.

How curiously linked to each other time and space can be; for that evening I spent with Chuck seems to be as long a one as I can remember. We laughed and joked with one another, enjoyed the fish that Chuck had prepared for supper, and which, as was always the case, was delicious in the extreme. Chuck began to sing a song from *Oklahoma*, and I joined in as best I could. We spoke of Aunt Dodo, and did imitations of her – or, rather, Chuck did – as she spoke of Molly washing her knickers – or, rather, of Bridget washing them for her. We spoke of certain films we had seen together, when we were at the hostel, and before we had even thought of sharing a flat together; and Chuck, once he became worked up, had a way of making me laugh uncontrollably, until I had to plead with him to stop. We only had beer to drink, and very little of it at that; but it seemed to quickly go to our heads; and by bedtime any cold-minded person might have judged us seriously drunk.

But within the space of that long and enjoyable evening, there seemed to be no room or place for George. Not once did I think of him; neither when I was having my bath; nor during supper. It was only when the evening came to an end, that his image found its way back to me: once Chuck and I had said goodnight to each other, and Chuck had switched off the lights (as he always did) and I was lying warm and cosy in my bed.

Whether I should have read something into that I was unsure. Did it mean, I wondered, that Chuck's hold over me was stronger than I had imagined? Or was it just the concentration of that one particular evening: because I had asserted myself with Chuck, and because there had been a temporary truce between us, as a result? I couldn't quite tell.

I only knew that as I settled down to sleep, it was George, not Chuck, that moved around in my head, and whose pale, northern eyes seemed to be smiling at me: and the smell of whose pipe seemed to be circling around my bed; and whose long, strong fingers seemed to be pressing upon my arm; and whose directness about his girl had so disarmed me.

The next day, I did take the unopened letter with me to the office – written, as you will remember, by the 'master' of the 'home' where I grew up, and whose name incidentally, and because I've not mentioned it to you before, was Mr Carson – and George rang me as he had promised to do; and did so at eleven-thirty in the morning, I noticed – the same time that he had rung me on the Monday. He sounded different: worried and anxious; saying that he hadn't slept very well, and asking repeatedly if I was all right, and whether I had had a row with Chuck. I told him that I had spoken to Chuck about his return from Scotland, but said nothing to him about Chuck having read his letter – partly because I didn't want to set Chuck and George against each other; and also, I suppose, because I had coped with the business of it so well.

We arranged to meet that very evening: this time, not at the office, but at the tube station at Knightsbridge; with plans to go on to a pub in Chelsea for a drink; and then to a local Chinese restaurant, which George was sure would be reasonable. I had told Chuck that I wouldn't be in that evening, and said that I was probably seeing George: to which he had responded quietly; just saying that it was no business of his, and that I must do what I must do. He had shown no signs of jealousy or of temper, and had even said to me, when he left for the City, that he hoped I would have a nice time. So I felt free and happy – and glad too in a way that I had no secret to guard any longer.

What I didn't know then, because there was no way that I could have imagined it, was what an important day this was to be for me; and not because of George – although, as it turned out, it did draw us closer together – but because the contents of the letter – the one that I had brought with me to the office – affected me so profoundly, and so dramatically changed my life.

It wasn't until the lunchtime that I opened it, and this is what it said –

Dear Richard,

Before you read this letter, do please let me make clear to you that you are in no way obliged to respond to it. Whether you do so or not is entirely up to you, since what it has to say, is bound to affect your life and affect your future.

So do please read it carefully and then think about it; and perhaps, if you feel a need to do so, come and see me and have a talk with me about it. I have a great deal of experience in such matters, and if you need guidance at all, feel sure that I can offer you some help.

I have been contacted by the head of our local constabulary, informing me that he has received a letter from a London solicitor concerning your whereabouts – and, indeed, your existence. No name has been given, of course, because, as you know, your name – Constable – is not a family one; but is simply the one that you were given by the nurses at the hospital, soon after you were discovered by a policeman when you were small. But it seems that the exact date and time of that discovery have been given, and for that reason the claim made by the solicitor could be true – which is that he is writing on behalf of someone – his client, that is – who believes that he is your father.

The solicitor's address is a good one, so the enquiry seems to be genuine; and he says that if your whereabouts could be traced, and if you could be informed of his address, then he would be pleased to meet you, and to give you further information.

He has added sensibly that he is perfectly aware that you may not care to respond, and that there could be reasons for your not wanting to meet your father, if the person he is representing should be that: but as I say, the date and time are so correct and so exact, that I can hardly think this isn't a claim well-founded; and that there isn't a possibility, at least, that you could now know who your father is – and your mother, too, no doubt; and perhaps discover as well, why it was that you were abandoned.

After all these years, I am sure that this is bound to come as a shock to you – as, indeed, it has been that to myself; but if you really wish to respond to it, then do please get in touch with me, so that I can help you with your decision, or give you the name and address of the solicitor – or both.

I am sure you will appreciate now why it was that I began my letter with such a caution. Things like this can cause a great deal of emotional disturbance, and I have no reason to think that you won't be affected strongly by it. So do please think about it carefully and, as I say, contact me. We would be pleased to see you in any case, if you cared to come down. You always write us such a decent letter, and my wife and I would take great pleasure in having you stay with us for a few days.

Yours, most sincerely,
and with all my very best wishes,

A. G. Carson

My first reaction was to think how pleased I was to be seeing George that evening, and that I hadn't arranged to see Chuck at the flat – which probably meant, I told myself, that I had a mistrust of Chuck: that I felt no confidence in the idea that he would be able to help me at such a moment; because I sensed, I suppose, that his feelings didn't really extend themselves to embrace those of another person – or didn't when they were disturbed, at least, as mine were that day.

All afternoon, I found myself thinking about the letter; wondering whether the claim it made could be true; and whether the enquirer really was my father; and if so, who he was or might be; and whether it meant that I had a mother as well, or whether they were divorced or separated – or, indeed, had never married: this last idea being provoked by the fact that, from what Mr Carson had written, it seemed that there had been no mention of her in the solicitor's letter. And I wondered too, why it was that I had been abandoned. That seemed such a savage action to have taken, and I felt such anger about it inside me – and always had done. But was there a chance, I wondered, of my now discovering the reason for it; and if I did discover it, would that reason perhaps make sense to me?

That evening, I arrived a little early at the tube station in Knightsbridge; and as I waited for George, found myself trembling; my lips quivering and my movements agitated: and George sensed as soon as he arrived, and as he came striding out of the tube, that something was wrong, or must have happened; for without saying a word, he took me firmly by the arm, and marched us across to a bus-stop, where we could catch a bus to Chelsea.

'Something's wrong, Richard,' he said. 'Don't speak about it. You need a drink. We'll go to a pub by the river where it will be quiet; and where we can talk . . . Are you all right?' he asked, showing the most genuine concern. 'You're not ill, I mean.'

I shook my head, fearing that if I attempted to speak I would stutter; and allowed George to get us on to the bus; and then, once we were in Chelsea, to walk us steadily down to the river.

The interior of almost any public-house is always a receptive space, I find; particularly in winter, when its gleam and polish seem so welcoming, and when it offers warmth and comfort, in the way that this one did by the river, on that bitter February evening. And with it being early, there were few people in the bars; so George was able to quickly order us a drink, and then to settle us down in a corner.

'What is it, Richard?' he asked immediately. 'What's wrong?'

I took out the letter and handed it to him.

He hesitated before opening it. 'You want me to read this?' he said, to make sure.

I nodded, still needing time before I could speak; and I observed George carefully as he began to read the letter.

I had told him nothing about my upbringing – I don't know why; and therefore knew that what was being said in the letter would be a surprise to him. So once he had finished it, it seemed no wonder to me that he should begin to read it again. And as he did so, and as my eyes rested upon his clean-cut, orderly features, and as I noticed for the first time, a small mole at the side of his forehead, memories of my past came flooding back to me. In that curious box of ours we call the brain, and whose time-scale seems to be so at odds with daily life, I experienced sounds and images from my childhood; hearing suddenly the voice of a small, dwarflike woman, with glistening, jet-black hair, and wearing circular, wire-rimmed spectacles, who, when I was six or seven, came to teach us about the Bible and to talk to us about Jesus; and who used to make us sing a song to prepare us for churchgoing, when we would pretend to drop pennies into a bag.

'Hear the pennies dropping,' it went . . . 'Listen how they fall . . . Every one for Jesus . . . He shall have them all'; which had always made me suspicious in some way; since, from my very first encounters with the New Testament, I had formed images of the Saviour that didn't include such things as money.

And I saw as well the long kitchen table in the 'home' – always so freshly scrubbed; and which, as it stretched itself from one doorway to another, used to appear, I always thought, to slope downhill; set, as it was, upon the rough, uneven stone floor, and against a row of enormous, black-fronted ovens, that ran the length of one whole wall; and that were always hot – even in summer; and from which, in the afternoons, a great series of tea cakes would be brought and placed rapidly upon the table, turned upside down to cool. Quite delicious cakes, I must add; some plain, some dotted with caraway seeds (which a number of the children disliked, but which I enjoyed immensely) and some – not many – thick with bright red cherries, or rich with juicy currants and sultanas.

I saw too, the small room that I had been given when I was older, and had just passed into my teens; and where, when the light was out, I would lie wondering who I really was, and why it should be that I was parentless; and had been given the name I bore, only because I had been found at night by a policeman; wrapped, I had been told, in a blanket, and stuffed roughly into a basket.

No wonder, I thought to myself, as I sat sipping my drink, and as George sat reading the letter, that the story of Moses meant so much to me; being placed, as he was, among the bullrushes; and then being discovered, of course, not by a policeman, but by a daughter of the great Pharaoh. I didn't think that *my* story could end like his, and that I might prove to be some great personage who would do something like lead the Jews out of Egypt; but I did have a kind of inkling in my mind that one day I would discover who I was, and that my parents would become known to me.

'This – 'em, Mr Carson . . .?' asked George, who by then had finished his second reading of the letter.

' – Is the master of the home,' I said – 'the children's home; where I grew up.'

'I think you should see him,' George said decisively. 'I'll go with you if you want me to: if you need support. I – I had no idea, Richard – none – that you were – well, you know –'

'An orphan,' I said.

'I was going to say "without parents",' said George, lowering his voice and speaking with care.

I feel almost ashamed to have to write this, but the concern shown for me by George had suddenly brought a tear to my eye, and I disliked myself for it. All my life, I had suppressed emotion of that kind, and tears to me were an indulgence.

'Thanks, George,' I said, 'for saying that; but if I do go, it'll be easier, I think, if I go alone.'

'But you will *go* – won't you, Richard?' he replied. 'You need to talk to someone with experience. It's difficult – or it is for me, at least – to imagine how it must be, to have grown up as you did, without a family; and with no knowledge of who you really are, or who your parents might be. So take my advice, Richard,' he said, stretching out his hand, and touching me on the forearm. 'Go this weekend. The sooner the better. The longer you wait, the worse it will be, you know . . . Is it far?' he said.

'No,' I answered, picturing the town where I grew up.

'It's just over an hour from London on the train – beyond Reading. A small town in the heart of the countryside' – which is what it was; with four main streets and a sturdy church at their centre.

You could be wondering, right now, what exactly the relationship between George and myself might be: whether we were in love with one another and heading for some kind of affair; or whether we were just using each other in some way, as I half suggested earlier. At that very moment – meaning, the one of that evening in the pub – I had no answer to that question. I was certainly aware of the fact that I needed George, and that he stood for me as some kind of stable, steadying figure, that I was perhaps seeking in myself. I'm not saying that I saw him in terms of some knight in shining armour, and that I had projections upon him of that kind; but I did think of him as a strength that I could rely upon; and just then, when my life was shifting, and seemingly changing so much, that naturally meant a great deal to me.

What I was unaware of though; and which I can now see was unfair of me; was how I had blinded myself to any shadow there might be in George; and had done so, no doubt, for reasons to do with convenience. That evening, for instance, I didn't once ask him about himself or about his feelings; or why it was that he had slept badly the previous night, and which he had told me about on the telephone, when he had rung me at the office. I totally accepted his concern for me, yet showed little for him in return. And as far as *his* projections upon *me* were concerned – well, I was aware that he would stare at me at times, in what I thought was a dreamy fashion; as if I was a great distance away from him; and this I can now see, could have been an indication of the fact that I was standing for him, perhaps, as some lost, waiflike – even retarded part of himself that he was needing to recover. Whatever, there did seem to be some very strong form of bondage between us, that enabled us to be quiet together; and in a way that I felt sure would be impossible with Chuck. When we left the pub, for example, and went on to the restaurant, we said little during the meal, and neither of us felt uncomfortable. I broke the silence only once, in order to assure George that I would follow his advice, and that I would try to see Mr Carson that weekend; but other than that, we were almost wordless.

Then, as we left the restaurant to walk home; going up one of those long impersonal streets that lead from the King's Road up to the Fulham Road, and then on through Pelham Street to South Kensington, the silence between us continued; and because of it, the intimacy between us deepened. At one point, as we passed beyond the glare of a street lamp, George slipped one of his arms around my waist and gave me a quick, affectionate hug; and I, in return, put a hand on one of his shoulders and gently tugged at one of his ears. Whether or not these small, physical gestures could have gone further, I cannot say – if, for instance, either of us had had a flat of our own that we could have used; since the fact was, that we had no place like that in which to be private. But if I am to be honest about it, I doubt very much that they would. We were happy together as we were, and if stronger expression between us was impossible – or would have been difficult, at least – it was certain that neither of us seemed disgruntled about it.

Chuck was waiting for me at home: half drunk, half naked, and stretched out upon my bed. I could literally smell him as I came in; and within a second of my entering, had seen him through the open doorway of my room; with his braces curled around his thighs, and his shirt wide open, and with it dragged down over his shoulders.

Instinctively, I braced myself – fearing trouble; and once I had closed the entrance-door, stepped quickly into the kitchen and ran the tap: partly to gain time; and also thinking that this would wake him. It wasn't a wise move, however, because he had obviously not been asleep, and had heard me when I came in; and when I turned from the kitchen sink, I found him standing immediately in front of me, his breath stinking of whisky, and his eyes as red as the eyes of a bull.

'So little Richard's come home,' he said. 'Come home to his Auntie Zee . . . Have a nice time – did he . . .? Out with his Georgie-Porgie?' He laughed quietly at me, and in a way that I thought was sinister.

'Yes, I did,' I said, wanting to be open, and to behave as if we were having a normal conversation. 'We had a drink in a pub in Chelsea; then supper in a restaurant . . . And George asked to be remembered to you,' I added, making a second false move.

'Georgie? Asked to be remembered to *me*?! . . . Like fucking hell he did! . . . Don't tell lies, Bobo . . . Don't!' he struck out at me, punching me savagely on the chest. ' – tell fucking lies! . . . Do you hear me? Don't *lie* to me, Bo!'

'Chuck, you're drunk,' I said, making my third false move, as I dodged past him to go to my room. 'I'm going to bed.'

'Going to *bed*!' he screamed. 'You're not going to bloody bed: not unless I *put* you there!'

I slammed the door of my room in his face, but this only provoked him further; and he came charging in, his shirt now hanging loosely from his waist, and his head swinging wildly from side to side.

Fortunately, it was then that I finally took the right action; for I simply turned to face him and stood firm; looking directly into his eyes, and touching him lightly upon the shoulder.

'You'd better get to bed, Chuck,' I said. 'You know what you're like when you've had a few too many . . . Come on,' I said. 'We're both tired and it's late. Do you want me to help you?'

By confronting him, and then by touching him in this way, his temper quickly changed; and he allowed me to guide him to his room. 'Now – can you manage?' I asked. 'Are you all right?'

He sat on the edge of his bed and looked up at me. 'Yes,' he said, letting out an enormous sigh. 'I'm all right.' Then, as he turned on to his side, and as I quickly covered him with blankets, he fell into a deep, drunken sleep; from which, thank goodness, he didn't wake until the morning.


# VII


I SEEM TO HAVE got a bit of a swell going in my story at last, and I am sure that you must be itching for me to get on with it. Before I do, however; or before I can, rather; there is something – two things, in fact – that I feel a need to speak about: things that I think I ought to have said but haven't.

One is an error, and is only a small one; but the other is more important, and has to do with meaning.

First, the error. You will probably remember my having said, quite early on in the book, that, unlike Chuck and myself, George didn't smoke. Yet, in a later scene in a restaurant, after we had been to see that Italian film at The Curzon, I have in fact shown him smoking a pipe. Then later again, in just the previous chapter, I have described experiencing the smell of his pipe in my fantasy, after that long evening with Chuck, and when I was lying warm and cosy in bed.

Now, what I really *meant* to say – and what I really *ought* to have said – was that unlike Chuck and myself, who smoked a lot (and inferring cigarettes, of course) George smoked a pipe and did so only occasionally. Now, that would have stressed a difference between us, and would have been sufficient to indicate that George was a less compulsive person than either of us; and that this was probably one reason why I had been so drawn to him.

Such a comment would have been in keeping with the period – meaning the 1950s – because people did smoke rather a lot in those days. So saying that about George would have been quite a good sign of his character. Yet the odd thing is (and this is a really stupid omission on my part) that whereas George, who was the more temperate one, has been shown having a smoke, Chuck and myself have not – not even once!

I have told myself that this is probably due to the influence of current fashion: that because it's not a 'done' thing to smoke these days, and is something that is frowned upon by medics, health experts and the like, I have allowed it to influence my writing. Yet if you cast your mind back to that time – or if *I do*, rather – there were no notices then, saying that smoking can damage your health; and in any film you might have gone to, the hero or heroine (Humphrey Bogart, for example, or Bette Davis) would have been seen smoking away like chimneys. So as I go on, I do think that at some point or another, either Chuck or myself – or even both of us – should be shown with a cigarette in our mouth.

Now for the other thing – which, as I say, isn't an error exactly, but has more to do with meaning; and which is connected with something I said about that book I bought in South Kensington, called *The Mystery of the Virgin*, by someone called Hewitt or Trewitt, I think it was.

Well, my first comment about it was that, as a result of reading that book, my mind – I think I said my intellect – became stirred or activated in a way that was unfamiliar to me.

Now, that's fine. We've all experienced that kind of thing – particularly when we were young: the sudden reading of something (a book, perhaps, as in this case, or even an essay) that will set our mind going; exploring new and unusual perspectives; ideas we had never thought ourselves capable of – that kind of thing. I've no quarrel with myself about having said that. But immediately after it, I dropped in the comment (and here I can quote myself, because I can remember it by heart) that the reading of that book – *The Mystery of the Virgin* – might 'partly be responsible for the writing of this book'.

Now, what did I mean by that, I wonder? I can hardly think I was simply saying that because my mind – or intellect, rather – had become activated in that fashion, way back in the 1950s – it had led, so many years later, to the writing of the book; because even if it had, it doesn't make much sense; and in my opinion, wasn't a thing worth saying at all.

I mean, there must be scores of people whose minds become stirred and activated in the way that mine had then been, yet it doesn't lead them to the writing of a book; unless, perhaps, it happened to have been some very touching tale or story they had read, that had become hooked on to their fantasy; and that they had then hung on to – maybe for years – and then eventually used: which we know wasn't the case with me, because it seems that that book, *The Mystery of the Virgin* had no story to it at all, and was simply a piece of non-fictional debate.

So my guess is that what I really meant to say was that it was a certain *understanding* gained from my reading of that book, that began to grow in me as a result; and that led, not to the actual *writing* of this one, because that wouldn't be true, but more to the *way* it is being written.

Yes: that, I think, is the point; and it is a point that is surely worth making; because it emphasises a certain philosophical attitude, and makes clear to the reader that the construction of this book, with its various asides, comments and so forth, is quite purposeful.

Anyway, since I didn't go into that, I think I'd better do it now. After all, I don't want to have readers picking at me – do I? – or things like that. And they could, you know; saying such things as that this book is all bits and pieces: that it appears to more or less make itself up as it goes along; and saying it moreover in a purely negative way.

What I feel a need to point out to you is that if you should find yourself thinking that, then you are quite *right* to be doing so, because the book is being written intentionally in that manner.

And this takes me back to what I was saying about the Virgin, and about the birth of Jesus: that what it symbolised – and what it still does, for that matter – was a sudden switch of emphasis, away from a God up there in the sky, to one that is not only down here, close to us, upon earth, but that is also actually *inside* us. That light and understanding come from *within*, not from without; is born, as one might say, out of darkness – even out of ignorance.

Now, that I think, is a modern understanding, and is in line with certain trends or aspects of psychology – with Jungian thought and so on. So it's worth pointing out, I think, that this book has been built brick by brick, as I believe I put it at one point, and has been drawn directly out of the material as it has presented itself.

So what needs to be said, I suspect, is that what seems to be going on here is something that is a little akin to the work of the alchemist – who, incidentally, was considered to be an artist; and that what I am doing is simply labouring patiently with the material and coaxing it towards a conclusion: adding, perhaps, that this is being done because it represents a new, more modern practice than, say, any form of premeditated or conceptual type of writing, in which everything is planned and plotted beforehand, and over which the writer presides in a godlike, omnipotent fashion.

Heads down, rather than up, could be a way of describing it; and brick by brick, or little by little, could be another.

There now. I've said my piece. I have done those things that I think I ought to have done, and hope there is some health in me, as a result.

So what will it be next, I wonder? Are we about to go off to the country, to meet the Carsons, or is there something else to pull out of the bag? Whatever, it is the material will provide it – that's for sure. And as for Chuck, I think I must tell myself as I go on, that I oughtn't to be too severe about him in my thoughts. After all, it was quite an event for him to be sharing a flat with me – as indeed it was for me; to be sharing a flat with him. And to be living close to someone – physically close, I mean – was a thing he had never imagined would be possible – and (although it is tragic to have to add this, I suppose) might not be possible for him again.

Chuck's condition – or his compulsions, rather, made any form of physical proximity appear as a threat to him, so I really do think that I must take that into account. I mean, we all have a part of ourselves that rather fears the flesh, and that can become ruled by it as a result; so tolerance and kindness is what's needed, however trying or difficult he proves to be.

Well. Thank goodness I've got *that* out of the way. And as we go on, I shall certainly show either Chuck or myself having a smoke from time to time; and I'll attempt to weave one such example of it into the text pretty soon. But as for what the next scene is to be, I can tell you for sure that it's not going to be a trip down to the country, to see Mr and Mrs Carson; because when I attempted to contact them on the telephone, to see if I could visit them at the weekend, I was told that both of them were away, and would be until the Monday – which meant that my meeting with them was delayed.

As you can imagine, I was rather put out by this. George had said to me that the sooner it could be arranged would be for the better; whereas now, I was being forced to wait for longer than a week before I could discuss with Mr Carson the contents of his letter. And to make matters worse, it turned out that George had to go off on a course, which he had told me was connected with his studies; and which meant that after that evening we spent by the river – first at the pub, and then at that restaurant where we had supper – I didn't see him for several days. Not, in fact, until the Wednesday of the following week. And since I had said nothing at all to Chuck about the business to do with my father ( and about the possibility I was then nurturing that I might even be meeting him in the near future) the time immediately ahead of me proved a most difficult one indeed.

I said to myself that I should do my best to be patient; and when he had telephoned me at the office to tell me about his course, George had said the same thing. However, it wasn't at all easy for me to be that. To begin with, there was Chuck to cope with, whose bouncy cheerfulness, once he had learned that George was to be away, proved almost too much to bear. So much so, in fact, that when the weekend arrived, it came as a relief to learn that he would be going off again with his friend, Darby – which meant that I was suddenly left free, and with the space of the flat to myself.

So we'd better pick the story up from there: from when Chuck had gone off with Darby for the day and I was left alone; and was beginning to go over the events of the past fortnight, during which so much had happened.

It seemed unbelievable to me that it should have been so short a time since Chuck and I had returned from Bognor Regis. So much in my life had changed. I had made what I now thought of as a true friend in George; had begun to realise that living with Chuck was going to be no easy matter, and that there seemed to be some kind of tension growing between us; had woken up intellectually to new avenues of thought that appeared to be making me grow; and had received a letter out of the blue, so to speak, that had turned my emotions upside down; making me believe, as it did, that I might at last have parents like everyone else; and that there could be a possibility, at least, of my soon meeting my father – and my mother too, perhaps.

The only thing that appeared to be niggling me right then – that is, beyond the general sense of excitement that I was feeling, was the sudden departure of George. He had told me that the course had come as a surprise to him, and that he had 'wished to hell' he could have got out of it; but it had made me extremely conscious of the fact that I knew very little about him; only that he hailed from Bonnie Scotland; had had a girl; was training to be an engineer; and was in the very final stages of his studies.

What *kind* of engineer, I had no idea – and that, I now realised was due to the fact that I hadn't asked: and also, of course, to the fact that so much had been happening to myself – and, moreover, that George had been more concerned and caring for me than I had been for him.

But what was bothering me now was this feeling I had that however genuine and true his concern for me had seemed; and however warm I had found his physical expression, whenever we happened to touch one another, if not in the impulsive action of that one kiss; there was something about him that I thought was rather shadowy. I couldn't describe it to myself in any other way. It was such a vague feeling that I had; and could have been caused, I tried to convince myself, by our not knowing each other as yet too well; and that I appeared, perhaps, to him, to be shadowy in a similiar way. Also that we needed more time, and that things had been against us; in that neither of us had a really private space of our own, and that there was always Chuck to be seen to and coped with. And even now, for instance, when we could have been alone together in the flat, George had made this unexpected announcement that he would be away from London himself.

However, I assured myself that time would sort it all out; and that I should be patient as George had said: and it was as I finally settled down to this idea that I heard a quick knock on the door; and answered it to find myself confronting a rather athletic, middle-aged woman, whose face seemed somewhat familiar to me.

'Is Chuck in?' she asked, giving me a nervous smile; and tossing her head back a little, as if she expected people to be put off by her.

'I'm afraid not,' I replied. 'Can I give him a message? He's out for the day with a friend.'

'Oh . . . No . . . Well . . . I'm his cousin – Molly. You must be his flatmate. You're Richard, I expect. You met my mother – didn't you – when you were down at Bognor?'

Suddenly I remembered where I had seen her face before – in some of those large, silver-framed photographs, that were placed about Aunt Dodo's room.

'Can I come in?' she asked, raising just one of her eyebrows, as if she couldn't be certain that I would say yes.

'Of course,' I answered, ' – do'; and as I stood back to let her in, she more or less sprinted past me into the flat, moving swiftly towards the kitchen and then veering on and into my room.

'This isn't Chuck's room,' she said, as I quickly followed her.

'No. It's mine,' I replied. 'How did you guess?'

'Oh, by the smell,' she answered, screwing up her dumpy little nose, that was so out of scale with the rest of her features. 'I can smell Chuck anywhere,' she said. 'He smells just like my mother.'

I had to laugh at this.

'Well, it's true,' she said, throwing her thick, leather pouch-bag on to my bed. 'I'm never sure which it is – the smell of a bear or of a lion; but it's certainly one of the two.'

I laughed again.

'Can I sit?' she asked, pointing at my chair. 'Can I smoke?' and before I could answer, had literally flung herself into the chair; and then – almost within the arc of that same movement, had stretched out a hand towards the bed, in order to fish some cigarettes out of her handbag.

'I'll get you a light,' I said, thinking that I would bring a box of matches from the kitchen.

'No need!' she cried, tossing a cigarette into the air and causing it to somersault before catching it in her mouth; 'I've got one here' – with which she seemed to conjure, as if from nowhere, an enormous, brass-plated lighter, that was shaped in the form of a pineapple.

'You smoke, Richard?' she asked, holding her cigarettes out towards me with one hand and lighting the one in her mouth with the other.

'Thanks,' I said, noting that the cigarettes were American.

'Light?' she asked, throwing her brass-plated lighter across at me.

I caught it, thanked her, and lit up; noticing that after the bravado entrance she had made, she had suddenly gone quiet; and that although she was smiling, her lips were trembling a little at the corners.

'Would you like a coffee?' I asked. 'There's some made. I had just finished my breakfast.'

'Oh, lovely,' she said.

'With sugar?' I asked.

'Yes. If you can spare it – lots.'

I went into the kitchen; reheated the coffee; and brought Chuck's cousin a mug of it.

'You know, Richard,' she said, as I came back into the room, 'you're quite a surprise to me. I never thought that Chuck would find someone decent; or someone even to live with, for that matter.'

'It's nice of you to say that,' I replied, 'but we're not together, you know. We're just friends – flatmates. We met in the hostel.'

'Oh,' she said. 'Trust *me* to get it wrong. I'm never right about anything . . . Sorry, Richard. That was clumsy of me – wasn't it?'

'That's okay,' I said. 'Jack thought the same thing.'

'Jack? – Oh, well, he *would*. What did you think of him? What did you think of Bridget?'

' – That they were brother and sister.'

'Who?' she said, screwing up her nose again, ' – Jack and *Bridget*?'

'Yes. They look so alike.'

She paused to think about this. 'Well, I suppose they do,' she said: 'but they're lovers – you know that, don't you?'

It was as she said this, that it suddenly struck me that I might find out from her what I had been meaning to find out from Chuck – how Jack and Bridget had met; and how they came to be working for her mother. I could see no reason *why* I should want to know this, but, none the less, I did; and I felt somehow that Molly wouldn't object to our having a gossip.

I won't go into the exact details of what was said; but in no time, I learned from her all that there was to know: which wasn't much; and which amounted more or less to the following: that Bridget had a sister, who, for a number of years, had been her mother's housekeeper and companion: that just recently, after a long and difficult illness, the sister had died; and that during this illness, when she had spent most of her time in hospital, Jack and Bridget had moved in to take her place. However, it seemed that for some reason (Molly's joke was the same as Chuck's, that they had made too much noise in bed) her mother had stipulated that if the two of them were to stay on, one of them must live out. And apparently – perhaps because it was a job that suited Jack's temperament; and perhaps too because it suited both of them in some other way – they had readily agreed to this.

Which meant that Jack lived in, and saw to the general running of the house – and, as we already know, took Chuck's aunt for her daily drives – and Bridget, who cooked and cleaned, and who came into the house each day, moved into a small fisherman's cottage a short distance along the coast. Quite where and when the two of them had met, or where and when they now made love, no-one seemed to be sure; but Molly was certain, as Chuck had been, that they were lovers.

So although their story was a little odd, there was nothing mysterious about it, as I was half expecting there might be; and as you, no doubt, were expecting there might be as well: but banal though it was, I knew that it was something I had been needing to know. At that point, my thinking this made no sense to me at all; but I clung on to it, none the less, in the way that one does with certain pieces of information; storing it swiftly away in some small cupboard of the mind. And because it was from her that I had gleaned the story, I felt rather warm towards Chuck's cousin. She wasn't aware, of course, that the questions I had put to her had been purposeful; but as she stubbed out her cigarette – saying that she was about to go down to Bognor, and that after a second smoke she would leave – I could see that my questions had made her nervous; because at one moment, she had pushed back her head, and had looked at me out of the corner of her eye. She didn't say to me, 'What do you want to know this for?' or some such question as that; but she might as well have done. And when she got up to say goodbye; and after she had stuffed her cigarettes into her bag; and had thrown her lighter into it as well; I must confess that I did feel a little uncomfortable.

Once Molly had gone, and after I had placed a note she had hastily scribbled for Chuck on a suitcase kept by his bed, I found myself thinking about the day that was lying ahead of me, and wondering what exactly I might do with it. Should I go to a film perhaps in the afternoon, and then on to a pub for a drink? Must I get some food in – or had Chuck left a supply? Did I need a bath or to wash some socks? Or should I perhaps go to the public library, to find myself something to read?

We had no fridge, but there was plenty of food in the house – stacked in a huge cupboard in the kitchen; and there seemed to be no socks that I thought needed a wash: and since I had had a bath just the previous night, I didn't think that one today would really be necessary. Which left either the cinema or the library. But neither of these appeared to be right; because none of the local films seemed at all interesting; and I didn't fancy a trip into the West End, to see what I knew Chuck would refer to later as 'more of that continental rubbish'.

And as for the library – well, I was becoming chary of the addiction I had to detective stories; and suspected that if I happened to find one there that appealed to me, I would become lost in it for the weekend.

So what I decided to do (and which was something I had been meaning to do for some time) was first to have an early bite of lunch, and then to walk down through Chelsea to the embankment.

As you know, I had studied architecture a little during my training as a surveyor; and I wanted to look at a number of turn-of-the-century buildings by the river: buildings by architects like Shaw and C.R. Ashbee, that were full of taut, mannerist proportions, and that were so impressive in their way. Then – once I had done that – I thought that I might take a stroll along Cheyne Walk; past its dark, elegant brick houses, that always appear so mysterious to me; seeming, as they do, to be so shaded by the past; and by the lives of those famous artists, writers and so forth, who, at certain moments in their careers, have lived in that area close to the river.

What I would do after that, I had no idea; but my pleasure lay in just being on my own again for a change, and in having no Chuck around me to cope with. If I felt tired, for instance, I could come back to the flat; or – if it suited me more – not come back to it at all. So I made no plans for the later part of the day; thinking to myself that I would simply follow my inclination. There was so much that I needed to digest, and to have been given a brief moment of pause (which I had at first found difficult to accept) now appeared as a welcome act of grace; as though the experience of leisure that it was offering was a thing I sorely needed.

I had put on my donkey-jacket to go out; because, with it still being February, I thought the air by the river might be cold; but it proved to be one of those days when the sun makes its first real presence felt in the year; and I found it warm enough to be able to remove my jacket and carry it over my arm. And as I strolled past those lofty, eminent buildings that had begun to engage my mind; and on from there, past those fine houses in Cheyne Walk, I found myself picturing the lives of their previous inhabitants: seeing them dressed in costumes of the past; seated at card-tables, perhaps, wearing gleaming silks and brocades; or at their desks, close to the tall, first-floor windows that looked across to the river.

There was much less traffic about then; and a stroll along the embankment wasn't the near-nightmare it is today, with diesel fumes choking the lungs, and the noise of the huge lorries from the continent threatening damage to the eardrums; so I was able to linger there for quite a while; pausing at times to sit on a bench by the statue of Carlyle, which is placed at the bottom of Cheyne Row; or to cross to one of the benches on the Embankment side of the road, which was then a relatively easy thing to do.

At half-past four, my stroll by the river had ended; and because it was already turning dark, I decided that I would take a bus back to South Kensington, in order to rest for a while at the flat. I had so enjoyed myself, meandering in those haunted, beautiful old streets, with the flat, grey river beyond – upon which a slow-moving barge might appear, its tar-black form broken by stripes of thick, sludgy-green paint, following the waterline of the vessel; and by small markings placed here and there in scarlet and mustardy yellows. It had so reflected my mood, that seemed to be floating and carrying me along. Not even the sudden departure of George had spoiled that moment of pleasure:

so that when I placed my key in the door of the flat, turned it and let myself in, it didn't exactly come as a surprise to me to find that all its rooms seemed so in order. And although I tried hard to do so, I could smell no trace of the presence of Chuck. Unlike his cousin, Molly, I obviously wasn't bound to him in any animal way: which made me realise that it was through my mind, more than through my body, that my relationship with him was maintained; and that, however tiring or strenuous this might be for me, it was only through a form of perpetual mental alertness that the life I shared with him was made possible.

That evening, after I had had a snooze and then a snack, and after I had washed myself and changed, I thought that what I needed most to do was to see people; and since I fancied a glass of beer as well, I decided to go to our local pub.

It was a Saturday night, and I imagined that the bar would be crowded – which indeed it was; so that, after I had nodded a brief good evening to the landlord, and had ordered myself a drink, I turned to see that the only seating available was at a small table in the far corner of the room, close to a side-entrance I seldom used, and opposite a sturdy, marble-faced fireplace, in which a fire was burning steadily – and which, with it being so warm for the time of year, was making that corner a little uncomfortable.

It was as I sat down that I noticed a man standing at the counter of the bar: a stocky figure of about fifty, with slightly receding hair and wearing a very ordinary, nondescript suit, who had unusually deep blue eyes that seemed to be staring directly at me.

He had obviously been there when I came in, and whilst I had been ordering myself a drink – and had taken me in, I presumed; or so it seemed; because he quickly came across to me, nodded, pulled out a chair that was placed at the opposite side of the table, seated himself, and said –

'You don't mind, I hope.'

I probably didn't reply to this, because he quickly turned his chair away from me – as if to say, I thought, that he wouldn't intrude unless he was welcome. So I said to him –

'It's quite warm, isn't it? – here by the fire.'

'It is,' he said without turning; 'but I'm glad of it. I've got no topcoat with me.'

It was only then that I noticed that this was so; and noticed as well (because he had been fingering it) that he was wearing a thick, gold ring that might have been a wedding ring; and which could indicate, I hastily told myself, that he might possibly be married.

We were then silent for a while, until he suddenly turned to me and said –

'Do you live in London?'

'Yes, I do,' I answered.

'Have you been here for long, then?' he asked, almost as if he knew that I had not.

'No,' I said, ' – just a few months. I live in a flat around the corner.'

Again we were silent.

'I'm only here for a week . . . It's a big place though – isn't it – London?'

'Huge,' I said.

'Bloody massive,' he answered with a laugh. Then he said, 'Come. Drink up. Have one with me.'

'No thanks,' I said.

'Why? You had enough?' he replied.

'I think so,' I said.

'Do you want to go, then?' he asked.

'I think so,' I answered a second time; and with that, finished my beer, gathered up my donkey-jacket and went out, using the small entrance-door, that was close to the table where we were sitting.

The air outside seemed surprisingly cold, after the stuffy heat of the bar; so I paused to slip on my coat. And as I did so, I noticed the blue-eyed stranger had followed me.

'Bit nippy,' he said.

'Mmm. It is,' I answered, pulling my coat closely around me.

'Shall I walk home with you, then?' he asked, in what I now recognised as being probably a Yorkshire or Derbyshire accent.

'If you like,' I said, not knowing whether I really meant my words or not, but feeling strangely warm and happy inside.

And in almost no time we were there; not just at the entrance of the building, but at the entrance-door of the flat: then stepping inside, but switching on no lights: then grabbing hold of each other; then tearing savagely at each other's clothes: then falling half-dressed, half-undressed upon the bed: then rapidly undressing each other further, and violently making love.

The sudden relief of this was enormous. I didn't care who my partner might be; where he had come from; whether he was married, single or what. All I cared about was that with the help of this stocky, blue-eyed stranger, whom I had met so casually in a bar, I had severed the knot of some psychic hold-up that had been bothering me for years. And as for George, I told myself that this might never have happened if he hadn't gone off on that wretched course; and that he should have been here beside me in London, at a time when I needed him most: when some dark secret to do with my past had suddenly broken free; and when, for a reason as yet unknown to me, it was now making its way towards me through Mr Carson's letter.

# VIII

'WELL,' said Chuck, as he came in, which was shortly after midnight and as I was about to go to bed, 'so how's our little Richard, then? Been on his owneeoh *all day*: with no Georgie-Porgie: no Auntie Zee – no nothing.'

He laughed uproariously as he said this, looking even more enormous than usual.

'I'm all right,' I answered, sensing a need to speak with care. 'I'm fine . . . How was *your* day, Chuck? Did you have a good one?'

'Did I have a *good* one?' he blurted back at me. 'Yes, of course I did. Fucking marvellous . . . What's the smell?'

'Smell?' I asked, caught out by him, as I so often was.

'Yes, smell. What's the fucking smell?'

'I don't smell anything,' I said.

'Well, *I* do,' he went on, sniffing the air suspiciously. 'You've had someone here – haven't you? Some *woman*.'

I was terribly relieved, of course, when he said this; and glad to be able to tell him about the brief visit of Molly.

'Molly!' he shrieked. 'What's *she* been doing here?'

'She just called. She just asked to see you – that's all.'

'Like fuck she did,' he said with a scowl. 'It's *you* she was after, Bo – not me. Dodo's put her on to you – that's what it is. They're a bloody pair. Anyone young: anyone new.'

'Don't be stupid, Chuck,' I said firmly, 'she just asked if you were in; and I gave her a cup of coffee.'

'I don't trust her,' he said. 'I never have done. She's sneaky. Always sticking her nose into other people's fucking business . . . What did she want?'

'I've told you – to see *you*, Chuck. We had a talk – mostly about Jack and Bridget and your aunt. She said she was about to go down to Bognor.'

'Well, you're lucky,' he said, 'that's what you are. She didn't ask you for anything, I hope ... Money, for instance; or something like that.'

'Of course she didn't. She had a cup of coffee; a couple of cigarettes – and then left. She scribbled a note for you. I've put it beside your bed.'

Chuck's attitude changed when I said this; and his voice deepened a little. 'I'll look at it later,' he said – meaning the note. 'I need a drink. I need a beer. Have one with me – come on. Tomorrow's Sunday. You don't need to be going to bed just *yet*, do you, for Christ's sake?'

I thought it would be wisest to agree with this; and followed him into the kitchen, where he opened a couple of bottles of beer.

'Don't trust women,' he said authoritatively, as we sat down at the kitchen table. 'They're all the bloody same. All up to tricks of one kind or another ... Cheers,' he said – lifting up his glass, and smiling at me in what I thought was a friendly way, and looking directly into my eyes.

'Cheers, Chuck,' I answered a little nervously, knowing how terribly strong his instinct could be; and fearing that he might be able to read into my expression how some person other than Molly had been with me in the flat.

'So,' he went on, 'did you have a nice day, Bo? Went to the pictures – did you?'

'No, I didn't,' I said, 'I went for a walk. There was nothing on I wanted to see – or not at the locals, at least – so I went for a stroll. In Chelsea: along the embankment.'

'Oh ... very *nice*,' said Chuck with a fixed smile, 'very healthy ... No wonder you're looking so well, Bo. All rosy-posey for a change.'

I blushed when he said this, and felt like kicking myself for doing so.

'There now,' he sniggled, 'our little Bo has got himself *all* flushed up in the face. Just because I said he was all lovely and rosy-posey!' – and he let out a great burst of his bouncy laughter.

' – So what you been up to then, Richard?' he suddenly asked; catching me out again; and speaking in a very pointed manner indeed.

'Up to? What do you mean?'

'Oh, come on, Bo! Don't give me that. You can't fool *me*. You've been up to *some*thing – I know it!'

'I've been up to *nothing*, Chuck,' I protested. 'I told you. I went for a walk – that's all: then had a drink at the pub.'

'Fucking liar,' he said scornfully, his voice now even deeper than before.

'I'm going to bed,' I said, not wanting to be drawn into his shadow. 'I'm tired ... you finish your beer, Chuck. I'll see you in the morning' – and with that, I swiftly rose from the table, in the hope of making my way back to my room; but as I passed the back of his chair he suddenly grabbed me around the waist and drew me back to him.

'Going to bed?' he said, laughing again, and looking up at me. 'Going to bed, Bo? Going to bye-byes?'

I tried to break free from him, but his grip made it impossible; so I decided that it would be best not to resist, and just see what would happen. Which, fortunately, was that he at once relaxed his hold; then slipped his hands down to my thighs; pressing them lightly at the back; as if to say that if I tried to break free from him a second time he would quickly grab me again.

'So what's our Bobo been up to, then?' he went on, with what seemed to be a sadistic curl at the end of his huge, curvaceous lips: 'Having a little wank, perhaps? Is that what it was? All on his owneeoh?'

As he said this, he let out a massive peal of laughter. 'Is

that what it was, Bo?' he continued. 'Is that what our Bobo was blushing about?'

'It's none of your business,' I retorted. 'I'm tired, Chuck. I'm going to bed.'

– And to my surprise, he suddenly let go of me, removing his hands from behind my thighs, as if to indicate that I was free.

'Well, *go* to bed, then,' he said, turning away, and taking up his beer. 'Just be your usual fucking self . . . It's typical of you – isn't it? Wanking yourself to death all afternoon; all on your owneeoh: then, when your Auntie Zee comes home, you've got no time for her; just wanting to go to bye-byes.'

'Look, Chuck,' I said, 'if you really *want* me to stay up with you, I will. I just thought that after being out all day with Darby, you'd be needing to get to bed yourself.'

'And *he's* no fucking different,' Chuck answered with a snarl. 'He's like you, Bo; another piss-arsed poker – *that's* what he is. Thinks only of himself . . . I don't care a shit: not about either of you . . . Get along now, for Christ's sake: get yourself to bed . . . I'll see you in the morning.'

And as he was saying this, he suddenly crossed the kitchen in order to fetch another beer. So I decided to use the chance he appeared to be offering and bolted into my room, half fearing that things still hadn't settled, and that he would soon be at me again.

However, this time I was wrong, because all I heard from him after that was a grumpy call he gave, just as I was dropping off to sleep, asking me 'what in the fuck' I had done with 'Molly's bloody letter'.

'It's by your bed,' I called back. 'It's on the suitcase.'

'On the *what*?' he shrieked.

'On the suitcase,' I repeated.

'Oh . . . The suitcase!' he shouted . . . 'Yes – I've got it!

'Nighty, 'nighty, Bo,' he added, almost with glee, 'I'll see you in the morning.'

'– In the morning, Chuck,' I echoed half asleep: then murmured, as if determined to have the last word: 'Do you know something, Chuck? Molly told me that you smelled just like your Aunt Dodo.'

'She *what*!' screamed Chuck, appearing briefly in my doorway.

'She said,' I said from my pillow, 'that you smell just like your Aunt Dodo.'

'The fuck she did,' growled Chuck.

'No, Chuck – it's true,' I said, 'honestly: and I don't think she was making it up.'

'You're nuts, Bo,' he answered, 'that's what you are . . . too much of that wanking – that's what it is. Get yourself to sleep now; and build yourself up – *that's* what you need . . . Smell like Dodo? Like bloody hell I do . . . You're nuts, Bo . . . I'll see you in the morning.'

The next day was a Sunday; and with it being one of our domestic days, all was bliss and calm; and in the evening, a kind of festival took place of Chuck's favourite songs. These included snippets from *Oklahoma*, of course; and 'Don't Put Your Daughter on the Stage' – a song by Nöel Coward which Chuck adored; and during which he assumed the role of Mrs Worthington, to whom the advice in the song had been given; miming shock and surprise, in conjunction with his singing, at all the outrageous, scandalous things that might happen to lady thespians. And from the delight of all that, and after the good night's sleep that followed, we moved forward into the new week without further outbreaks between us.

For once, it looked as if the life I shared with Chuck had achieved a kind of balance; and on the Monday, when he went off to the City, dressed in his well-cut suit, and his only slightly flamboyant tie; and with the fine quiff that he shared with his aunt swept boldly back from his forehead; he looked more like some elegant city stockbroker than just an ordinary teller in a bank. In fact, so taut was his mask – so impeccable – that no-one passing him in the street could have guessed how wild he was inside: although, having said that, I think that when he dressed himself in that fashion – in his city uniform, so to speak – he emitted some curious kind of glow: and that because he had at least faced, and had at least *attempted* to come to terms with, some compulsive side of his being, he must have appeared more radiant – and more exotic too, perhaps – than most of his fellow workers.

Just two days later – on the Wednesday – George returned to London; and because we had arranged it before he had left, was meeting me at the office at about six. And as I sat waiting for him to arrive, I noticed how tense my mind had become: not so much on account of George, or because of a certain question lurking in my mind concerning the truth of where he had been; and why it was that he had left London so suddenly; but more because it was now so much closer to the Friday when I would be leaving for the country, and because I felt so challenged by the decision that I knew must be part of that visit.

My mental state just then must have been similar, I suppose, to that of the long-term prisoner who is about to be released; and who, although he is excited by the idea that he is on the point of obtaining his freedom, is at the same time living in fear of it, and clings to what he is familiar with, the sequestered life of his cell.

All my life I had been without parents; which meant that it was an important part of my reality. Whereas now, because of that message from Mr Carson, I was conscious that this could change; and one side of me seemed to be resenting it. Better the known than the unknown, might be a way of describing it, perhaps; which was probably why I had checked myself from projecting too much upon the outcome of that visit. For instance, I hadn't once risked dashing ahead of myself in time, as if to some imaginary point in the future, when I might be meeting my parents in person. Nor had I speculated, as I possibly might have done, as to whether they might be rich or poor, or whether they might be fat or thin; or whether they had perhaps suffered some great tragedy; and that this would provide a reason for their having abandoned me as they did. But I came close to doing it, none the less; which was probably the cause of my anxiety. What I was needing most to do right then was to arrive at the point of a decision; to have discussed with Mr Carson the question of whether I should choose to contact my parents; to have reflected upon what he had said; and then to have acted or not acted, whichever the case might be.

So with all these various thoughts and ideas spinning around in my head, and with all this constant checking of my projection, it meant that when George suddenly arrived (tapping lightly upon the window-pane; because he had seen me from the street; and because he had noticed that no-one was with me) it came as something of a shock. So much so, in fact, that I wasn't sure at first that it was him. For one brief second, I took him to be some quite different person entirely. He looked so light; so full of good cheer; and was waving his hands at me in an almost comical fashion, as if he wasn't quite sure that he would be recognised; almost as if – in relation to myself, I mean – he wasn't too certain of his identity.

'Richard!' he exclaimed, as I invited him into the office. 'Richard – how are you?'

I looked hurriedly into his eyes, but could read no trace of any shadow. He seemed so genuinely delighted by the idea that we were meeting each other again. With the result that I never once questioned him, as I had half intended to do, as to what his course had been about; or why it was that he had gone off as he had done so suddenly; and was pleased to slip back without pause or interval into the habitual pattern of our relationship. And if there was some truth about him that was unknown to me; and that my imagination seemed to be telling me might be lurking somewhere in the background; then it was something which I, at that very moment, wasn't too anxious to explore.

This reluctance was perhaps due partly to Chuck: that because the life we shared in the flat was full of such startling changes and contrasts, that it seemed at times to be almost tempestuous, I was only too thankful to have the opposite – and to have found it, it seemed, in George. Whatever, I knew that the pleasure I felt that evening couldn't possibly be an illusion. I cannot deny, of course, that there weren't occasions – and particularly on a Sunday – when I didn't enjoy Chuck's outrageous company; but it was as if there was some part of me (one that was linked to cautiousness, I suppose) that felt so much more comfortable with George.

This could have been a kind of narrowness, perhaps; and due to some fear I had of the full richness of life; and it was probably why I had been disturbed, now that I come to think of it, by Mr Carson's letter. It was as if one side of me clung to a life based upon habit, similar to that of a prisoner in his cell; whilst another longed to have a release from it, and to be in touch with things that were irrational. Which was why, of course, when Chuck and George were away, it had acted as such a release for me when I met that blue-eyed stranger, and we had so violently made love.

As yet, it seemed that I had found no path between these two opposites, and was tending to veer from one extreme to another: in which I was totally unlike Chuck, who, as I had witnessed at Bognor Regis, when he had knelt naked before the fire, and when he had expressed to me his philosophy, that 'you might as well be happy with it', was totally conscious of the fact that, however possessed he might be on occasions by the sheer giganticism of his physique; and however turbulent this might make him, because the force of it was so strong; it was none the less a truly central part of his make-up, and was therefore something that he must live with.

Whether or not George was like me in this respect I wasn't exactly sure; but if I look back at that time, then it seems to me that he was as unsure of himself as I was; and that what we enjoyed most in each other's company was the sharing of some protective, dreamlike, fantasy-world, rather than the more self-conscious sides of our beings.

Because I had never been alone there when he had called, George hadn't been into the office before; so, rather than discuss what we should do with our evening in the street, I suggested that we sit for a while at my desk. The weather still wasn't warm, and it was already almost dark; and although now empty, the office wasn't at all unwelcoming or uncomfortable, as such places can be at times. So that is what we did. George took out his pipe and I my cigarettes, and we lit up; each sitting in a chair beside my desk, and with the rest of the office in shadow.

'Well, Richard – how have things been?' George asked, once we were settled.

'Oh – up and down,' I replied.

'You mean with Chuck?'

'Yes, mainly. Some days he's all right. Others – well, he's a bit of a trial.'

'That's what I was thinking when I was away,' George

said. 'Chuck's a very unsettled person – isn't he? It can't be easy, Richard, to be living with someone like that.'

'You're right. It isn't,' I replied.

'Then why do you do it?'

'Why? Well, just because I do. It was Chuck's idea that we share, and I fell in with it, I suppose.'

'Perhaps you did,' said George, 'but you could change that – couldn't you – if you really wanted to?'

'How?' I asked, since this was a thought that had never occurred to me.

'Well – by leaving, of course.'

'Leaving?' I answered, my voice lifting, and trembling perhaps as well.

'Yes. You could leave. Get out. Go somewhere else . . . I mean, if it's difficult, and if it's dangerous, too – which I sometimes think it is – you could just go.'

As George was saying this, I became genuinely astonished at my reactions. What he was saying was so simple and direct, and made such sense to me, I would have thought that it would have come to me as a relief. And yet the effect it had was quite the opposite. For I found myself almost quaking at the idea that I might be making such a move. That was the surprise for me – and the challenge for me as well: but I said nothing of this to George, because I was sure he would find it illogical; and all I said to him in reply was that there was no place to which I could go.

'Well,' he answered, letting out a well-rounded puff of smoke, 'you could think of sharing with me, for instance. What would you say to that?'

'With you?' I asked, somewhat dumbfounded.

'Yes – with me. What would you say to it, Richard? I can't stay in that hostel forever; and once I start work, I shall need a flat of *some* kind – shan't I? So what do you say?'

'I don't know,' I replied, 'I –'

'Look, Richard,' he said, allowing another puff of yellowish smoke to emerge from between his teeth, 'I'm sorry. I've rather sprung that on you – haven't I?'

'You have,' I answered, in an uncertain fashion; and glad to be freed from the confrontation.

'Well, just forget it then,' he said – 'or do so for the moment, at least. You've a lot on your plate right now, what with the business of your parents – or parent, or whatever. How is that affecting you, by the way? Are you still thinking of going to the country, Richard, to see mister – whatever his name was?'

'Yes. Mr Carson,' I said, filling the name in for him.

'Oh, I see,' he replied. 'Well then, we'd better not speak about what I just said, until that is over and done with . . . Do you think you will pursue things, Richard – with regard to the solicitor's letter, I mean? Have you any ideas about that? Do you want to meet your father, for instance – presuming that the person in question is that?'

I paused before I replied: then said to him, 'I don't know, George. I feel – well, I don't know *what* I feel.'

And that was the truth of the matter. Right then I didn't know what I felt about anything; neither about Chuck nor about George; nor about whether I wished to have parents like everyone else; nor about my sharing a flat with George – which, as with so much of what had been happening, had come as such a surprise to me.

What I was really wanting to do just then was to think about nothing at all. And had both Chuck and George been away; and I had met some other stranger in our pub; then what would have made me happiest at that moment would have been to curl up beside him in bed. Whereas, what I had to settle for was another of those long, meandering evenings with George; during which, as I can now see, I would in some way draw upon his strength – and which he, in turn, seemed to take pleasure in. And at the end of it, return to the life that I shared with Chuck; keeping my wits about me as I did so; knowing that I must be prepared for almost anything. And knowing as well, of course, that in just two days' time I would be leaving London myself; catching a train from Paddington to Reading; and then a bus with which I was familiar, to the small town where I grew up; and where, in a spacious, Georgian mansion, that had been converted into a 'home', I would discuss with Mr Carson the contents of his letter.

On the Thursday, I met George again. No mention was made of his proposal that I should move, so the eve of my departure was an untroubled one. What George and I did that evening, I cannot remember; except that I know we walked for a while in the streets, because it was good to be out of doors; and we probably had supper together in one of those cheap, bistro-style places that were becoming popular in those days, which offered such things as chicken served in a basket. Or it could have been in a converted garage, as I remember it, not far from the Brompton Road, where the tables were covered by gaudily coloured oil-cloth, and lit by candles stuck into bottles; and where a plate of deep red beetroot soup, followed by a delicious serving of beef stroganoff, would have cost us practically nothing.

What we talked about, I have no idea. That is one of the peculiar things about our relationship: that whereas with Chuck I can recall, and often without effort, almost whole evenings of our talk; with George it is the reverse; in that only brief snatches of what he would say to me appear to have fixed themselves in my mind. This might be due to the fact that Chuck both alarmed me and amused me so much and because he used so many expletives. Or was it more, I sometimes wonder, because there was something very 'actorish' in his make-up, that made all his words seem part of some 'show' – so that, although the various scenes he made were truly genuine ones, there was, none the less, a side of his personality that was more self conscious than one might think; and which meant that, to a degree, at least, his different shifts and changes of mood were part of some carefully judged performance.

At any rate, that was certainly the impression he gave that evening after I had said goodbye to George. For when I came in, I found him warbling away at the kitchen sink, where he appeared to be washing up his supper things; wearing a mammoth, canary-coloured sweater that had two protrusions upon the chest, and that were meant to be women's breasts; a towel wrapped turban-like around his head; and, apart from a pair of coarse but spotless under-pants, which seemed to be partly composed of string, no form of clothing whatsoever upon the lower half of his body.

'Hello, sweetheart,' he called out, using it as a chummy form of endearment he seemed not to have exercised before, and that he had probably heard the conductors use on the buses. 'Have a nice time – did you? Been out with your Georgie-Porgie?'

'Chuck,' I answered, 'you're the limit.'

'The *limit*?' he said, with what was meant to show surprise. 'Now, what *do* you mean by that . . . ? Just because it's Amami night, and because I've got a towel wrapped around my head?' (I must explain perhaps that 'Amami' was a popular brand of shampoo that was much advertised in those days; and that, although this was a Thursday, of course, the expression 'Friday night is Amami night', was one that more or less passed into the language.)

'No, it's not just the towel, stupid,' I said. 'It's *every*-thing!' laughing at the sight of him in his gear.

'I don't know *what* you mean,' he replied, flicking his dishcloth at me, and sending a spray of water across the room, 'I am looking *perfectly respectable* . . . I hope you're not laughing, Bo, just because I've got no trousers on; because there's *nothing funny* about that . . . Look,' he said, swinging his hips to one side, and thrusting his great hunk of backside towards me, 'they're the best pair of legs in London . . . they're like Betty Grable's,' he added with a false snigger, 'they go *all* the way; from the heel right up to the bottom.'

Both of us roared at this, and it set him going again; now singing songs like 'Kiss the Boys Goodbye', or 'The Fleet's in Port Again', or one with the words, 'Cuban rum and towels from the very best hotels', which Chuck always enjoyed, and which – because of the word 'Cuban', I suppose – he always sang in what he would boast of as his 'Latin-American rhythm': and with him totally conscious of the fact that he held me captive under his spell, and that there could be no hope of my getting to bed until his outrageous performance had ended.

Nothing nasty occurred. He didn't tease or taunt me about George. But at one point, when he paused to adjust his 'boobs', as he insisted on calling them (and which he was later keen to point out to me were just two pairs of his 'dirty, rolled-up old socks'), I noticed that a tear had formed in his eye. Was it due to our laughter, I wondered; or was it perhaps that by means of that cunning, powerful instinct of his, he had sensed that things were beginning to change; and that due to events as yet unknown to him, our relationship was ending?

The next morning, I was busy packing a small suitcase that I intended taking with me to the country, and had said nothing at all to Chuck about the real reason why I was going. I had got up early, because I was catching a train immediately after work, and I wanted to take the suitcase with me to the office: and Chuck had come to my room and was watching me from the doorway.

'Don't forget your toothbrush, Bo,' he said, speaking quietly, and with what I thought was a hint of sadness in his voice.

'Don't worry,' I said, 'it's all here. Brush, soap, blades; razor – everything.'

Chuck hadn't yet changed out of his pyjamas, and was rocking gently from side to side; which seemed to indicate that he was nervous; so I said to him, 'I shall miss you, Chuck,' not meaning it quite in the usual way; and which was insincere of me, I suppose. 'But I shall be back on Sunday, you know . . . I did tell you that – didn't I?'

'You did,' he replied, his voice still very low in key. 'If I'm out, Bo, I'll leave you something: one of my soups, perhaps; in case you're cold.'

'Thanks, Chuck,' I answered a little sharply, not wanting to stir up too much sentiment.

'Oh, it's nothing,' he said, falling into a glum kind of silence, and half staring at me with those enormous, saucer-shaped eyes of his, that so reminded me of his Aunt Dodo's . . . But then, as I was on the point of locking my case, he suddenly pounded across the room.

'Silly, billy!' he shouted. 'You've left your tie hanging out! . . . Here; let me *see* to it for you, for goodness sake.'

I looked at my suitcase, and saw that part of my tie had indeed been caught by its lid – and both of us laughed, breaking the tension between us.

'Bo,' said Chuck, now standing close to me, 'you're not short – are you?'

'Short?' I answered, not understanding him.

'Yes. Of cash, I mean. I drew some yesterday at the bank, just in case you needed a little extra.'

'Oh, thanks a lot, Chuck,' I said. 'No, I'm not short. I'm careful. I can manage. And I don't expect to be spending much in the country.'

'Look,' he said, suddenly taking a five-pound note out of his pyjama pocket, 'I want you to have this, Bo. Not as a loan; but as a present, I mean.'

'But I don't *need* it, Chuck,' I said, 'honestly, I don't. It's kind of you, but –'

As I began to protest, however, I saw how hurt he was by the idea that I was refusing to take his gift; so I instantly changed my mind; and said, feeling somewhat embarrassed, 'Well, it's jolly decent of you, Chuck. I appreciate it a lot.'

– And it was with that hesitant exchange between us in mind, that I left that morning for the office. Was it Chuck's means, I wondered, of assuring himself that I would be returning to the flat; and because he had sensed, perhaps – as he seemed to sense so many things, that there was some different reason for my departure than the one that he had been given?

Whatever, it took until the guard had blown noisily upon his whistle, and the train on which I was travelling had begun to chuff its way towards Reading, before I was able to concentrate, in the way that I felt a need to do, upon the true purpose of my visit.


# IX


'NOW, RICHARD, help yourself to vegetables,' said Mrs Carson. 'There are peas, cabbage, potatoes – and roasted parsnips too; a favourite of yours, as I remember.'

'You remember everything, Emma,' her husband remarked with a happy smile on his face, as he turned from a rather institutional-looking trolley that had been trundled into the room and that he was using as a sideboard.

'Do I, dear?' Mrs Carson answered with a laugh. 'Well then, it's just as well, perhaps . . . It's a long time since you were here, Richard,' she added; abruptly changing the subject. 'We'd almost given you up, you know – hadn't we, Alec?'

'Well, not exactly, Emma. He has always kept in touch with us by letter: and very nice ones too, I must say. You have quite a talent there, Richard.'

'Oh, yes, your *letters*, Richard,' added Mrs Carson: 'they're always so lively! I do wish *I* could write like that.'

'You write very well, Emma; so don't run yourself down. Is that enough meat, Richard – or shall I carve more?'

I assured him that what I had on my plate was plenty; and began to serve myself with the various vegetables that were set at the centre of the table where I was sitting with Mrs Carson; and that was placed within the curve of a large bay window that faced towards the garden, and which in daylight, gave a view of the town beyond.

Now, of course, the curtains were drawn; and behind us a fire burned steadily in a large, open-style fireplace, which had a fine period surround, and which gave the room a feeling of ease and comfort; and this in spite of the fact that beyond a square of rather ancient-looking carpet, the floor itself (which was probably parquet, I thought) had been covered with a kind of bluish-grey linoleum, that was highly polished; but that reflected the few lamps that were placed here and there, and – from the table where we were sitting – was catching the deep red glow of the fire.

'Have you ever thought of writing, Richard?' asked Mrs Carson suddenly. 'From what we can gather, you don't seem to have settled down to what you were trained for, in spite of doing so well at it all at college. Why is that, I wonder? Is it the wrong type of work for you, perhaps? Not that writers make much money – if you were to become one of those, I mean – unless they write women's books, or something like that; or detective stories – that kind of thing. But it's wonderful to have a gift, you know. I suppose I might have taken up words myself, had I remained single. And if I *had* done, I think I'd have gone in for something rather mechanical – like Agatha Christie, I mean. I don't imagine that I could have written romantic novels, because I'm not a romantic person – am I, Alec? I'm too matter of fact ... What kind of books do you *read*, Richard? The classics, perhaps? The old ones, I mean? Or more modern things, like Lawrence? Have you read him? He's a favourite of mine; though his writing is hardly what you would call mechanical – is it?'

'No, it certainly isn't,' said Mr Carson. 'He's a romantic – Lawrence: all passion and colour. Very little form, I think. What do you think, Richard?'

I had to tell them that I had as yet read only *The Rainbow*, and that it wasn't exactly the kind of writing I enjoyed; and then added, a little sheepishly, that what I really liked was detective thrillers.

'Oh, my!' said Mrs Carson, 'You surprise me, Richard. I couldn't see *that* in you, you know. Now I wonder why that is? I've just said that I would like to write that kind of thing myself; yet oddly enough it's a type of book that I seldom read – which doesn't make much sense, does it? Perhaps Lawrence supplies the passion I lack in my life – or in my soul, rather,' she added with a laugh. 'Is that true, Alec, do you think?'

Mr Carson laughed with her in return. 'You speak as if you were a cold person, Emma. You aren't exactly passionate, perhaps; but you are far from cold. And you can certainly be ardent at times – about books, for example. That is such a favourite subject of yours; and you are looking for an ally there in Richard, I suspect; because I read so little myself.'

'Yes. I do love books,' said Mrs Carson, in her light, silvery voice. 'I love their words. They are more definite than talk, which I like almost as much; because you can always look them up – can't you? I've just been reading Jane Austen, for example –'

'– Now, dear,' said Mr Carson, intercepting, 'you must keep that for later, or our supper will be cold . . . Here, Richard,' he said to me, as he joined us at the table, 'there is plenty more of that mint sauce, if you care for it. Come along now. Tuck in. You've eaten little since lunchtime, I suspect . . . Emma, pass the parsnips – will you? Richard's not the only one to like them, you know. They're not nice boiled; but roasted – ah! It's one of the finest dishes in the world!'

The conversation continued like this throughout supper – veering from time to time towards literature; and mixed in with snatches of gossip about the town and about their 'children', as they spoke of them, which included myself, of course; and also with the chiming of a clock, placed upon the mantelpiece, which marked each quarter of the hour; the pendulum of which consisted of three purple-coloured balls that were set in brass; and that revolved slowly beneath the clock-face: the whole of which was contained in a tall glass dome.

I so enjoyed that supper. After the build-up to the weekend, and the various ups and downs there had been with Chuck, it was a great pleasure for me to be sitting in such a very ordered atmosphere; and to be eating in such a civilised, sensible manner. And I had quite forgotten how charmingly light the Carsons could be; and noticed how careful they were not to impose themselves upon me; and in allowing me to enter their world in a very gradual way, by not demanding that I participate in it immediately, and being content at times to talk to each other as they would normally; not excluding me, but only gradually drawing me towards them so that I couldn't help wondering why it was that I'd kept away from them for so long.

At nine o'clock we had finished supper; and as the clock chimed the hour, Mrs Carson left the room, explaining that she had her duties to attend to, and that she must do her evening 'round', as she spoke of it; which I knew meant checking to see that the smaller children were in their beds, and the older ones, who were in their teens, were either in or out, according to whatever arrangements had been made. And as she passed my chair, she paused to smile at me and to pat me upon the shoulder; as if to let me know, I thought, that although she had no children of her own, she had none the less mothered enough of them; and that if I had delayed my visit for so long, it was merely a part of my growing up; and was nothing that I had a need to feel self-conscious about.

As soon as she had gone, Mr Carson suggested that I help him to clear away the supper things; and that if we stacked them carefully upon the trolley and then pushed it into the hall, it would prevent our being disturbed. 'Then we can have a little talk, Richard,' he said, '– by the fire; since that is what you came for. And then, if you feel it is necessary, we can talk again tomorrow.'

I must admit that I hadn't been expecting this, and for a moment felt caught out; but I quickly steeled myself to it, all the same: though I have to confess to you that as we sat in chairs at either side of the fire, I still felt a strong tension in my stomach; and at one moment, half feared that I might vomit.

For most of you who are reading this book, and who have had parents all your life, my saying this might cause some astonishment. Perhaps to *your* mind, I ought to have been both pleased and curious about discussing such a subject – the one, I mean, of whether I should choose to contact my parents; and because of that, my fear might seem somewhat puzzling. But what you have to imagine is how huge a difference it makes, to have never seen, nor to have even heard of, the two people who brought you into this world; and the physical closeness of someone, who, in one way or another, was likely to resemble myself, was rather frightening for me.

What you have to remember is that I had always been on my own; and that however kind and caring Mr and Mrs Carson had been, and however fond of them I might be, there was no bond of blood between us; no deep ties or roots of that kind. And I think it probable that people who do have parents, take all that intimacy too much for granted: though there must be times, of course, when they dislike the mental and physical closeness of such a relationship; and the element of incest that is implied by it is bound to be a difficult thing to cope with – and, if it is played out at all, is bound to lead to family dramas of one kind or another; and is indeed the stuff out of which so many books and plays are formed.

Until then, my life had lacked the possibility of that particular kind of drama; and in a way, I suppose (in that there seemed to be danger in it, mingled with what I can only call some odd brotherly kind of love) the closest that I had yet come to it was through my relationship with Chuck.

But now, of course, all that could be different. Now,

instead of being on my own, there was at least a chance that I would be meeting someone with whom I shared the same flesh, the same blood – perhaps even the same looks and the same temperament; and that form of closeness made me nervous.

More than anything, this may have been because the feeling it was generating was so new to me: and perhaps that very newness was the reason why I was experiencing at that moment what appeared to be a bout of nervous hysteria. And it could have been that Mr Carson was aware of this; for as we began our talk, I noticed how slow and ponderous he was about everything: first going to a drawer and bringing me the solicitor's letter; and then, before we began to discuss it, allowing me to read it and to relate to it quietly.

The contents of the letter revealed nothing other than what Mr Carson had already told me: that the solicitor was writing on behalf of someone who believed himself to be my father, and that the reasons he gave for this were that he knew my sex to be male; that he was able to give the precise date (and almost the precise time, it seemed) on which I had been abandoned; and because he knew as well that I had been deposited upon the entrance steps of the police station to which the solicitor was writing. And it said too, that if I could be traced, and if I cared to contact the solicitor's office, further proof would be available.

Having the letter in my hand, and being allowed to read it without interruption, reduced the tension in me considerably – and, very much to my surprise, I found that I had already come to a decision. I said nothing of this to Mr Carson; but as I handed the letter back to him I knew inside myself that as soon as I had returned to London I would be ringing the solicitor's office and asking for an appointment; and that, however upsetting such an idea had seemed just a short while ago, I now knew for certain that it was a direction I would follow.

There is little point in my relating to you the details of what was then said. You will have enough of an impression of Mr Carson to know that the advice he gave me was sensible, and was offered with a considerable amount of care. He warned me, for instance, that after a time I might feel angry: that if I decided to respond to the solicitor's letter, and make a first move towards my father, it might be more with a feeling of resentment than I as yet realised. As he pointed out to me, the fact that my surname was not a real one, and that, in this respect, I was different from other people, was bound to have affected me over the years, however used to it I had become; and however difficult it might be for me to imagine that I had a right to any other.

He said too that stories such as my own weren't always blessed with a happy ending: that I might dislike my parents, for example – or they might dislike me: though he quickly added to this that he had certainly known one such case of reunion that had gone 'swimmingly', as he had put it, and which had ended with 'smiles all round'.

So by putting both points of view, he did his best to prepare me for what I knew now lay ahead. He also pointed out that the reason for my being abandoned might be a complex one: that there might be some mystery attached to it: something that I couldn't possible foresee; and that that in itself might not only explain things to me, but could also help me to make my amends more easily.

'People do all sorts of things for all sorts of reasons, Richard,' I remember him saying. 'Your parents may have quarrelled, for instance, or separated; or perhaps one of them had been gravely ill – or even both of them . . . You must be open about it; clear your mind,' he said, 'try not to have ideas . . . If you should decide to contact this person who claims that he is your father, go towards it with an open heart and an open mind. That way, you will find it all less troublesome.'

'Now,' he said, rising from his chair, 'I think you and I should have a little nightcap, perhaps. A little elderberry wine is what I was thinking of. It'll make you sleep like a top. Or there's ginger, if you prefer it – or even, let me see . . .' he said, opening a glass-fronted cupboard and peering into it, 'if you don't care for that type of thing, I can offer you a nip of Scotch. How about that?'

I said that the elderberry would be fine, remembering that I had drunk some once at a Christmas party, and that it had a curiously dark, potent taste that I seemed to like. And thinking too that it was probably something Mr Carson had made himself; and because of that would be pleased. And after a while, Mrs Carson returned from her rounds and joined us; surprising me by saying, 'Oh, none of those country wines for me, Alec. They're a real fad of yours. If I have anything, it'll be a little whisky and water. It's good for the heart – isn't it? Just a sip – no more: though it's best, you know, with hot water and sugar. That's one of the most comforting drinks I know.'

In that way, the evening ended; and I made my way to my room, which was over the kitchen; and which was the one I had been given whenever I had come home on holiday from college – which I realised was the last time I had actually lived in the house.

I had no particular affection for it. It's true that what little furniture there was had remained the same, and was placed in exactly the same position; but there was nothing in or about the room that allowed me to think of it as my own – so it was a kind of abstract space in a way, and was probably why, as I began to undress, I felt a little shy of myself;

almost as if I had been in a public changing-room of some kind – at a swimming-pool, for example; or more probably, in one of those cubicles at a hospital where you are asked to remove your clothes, before the consultant comes to inspect you; and I changed into my pyjamas much more hurriedly than I ever did in London, in the flat.

But what it made me so conscious of was how, in this respect, Chuck's influence upon me had been positive; in that I no longer had inhibitions about my nakedness, in the way that I seemed to have had when we had first moved in together. I'm not saying that either of us ever walked freely about the place in the nude; but we certainly didn't hurry about changing our clothes, or about rubbing ourselves down after a bath, or anything like that: and that was a new freedom for me, which I now saw that I should value.

And as I settled down in my bed, with the curtains half drawn back, and with a view beyond them of a deep indigo sky – broken occasionally by a furtive winter moon, and the twinkling pinpoints of a few stars – I knew for sure that home for me was more those few rooms that I shared with Chuck, close to the temples of Art and of Science; than it was here, in the country, where I grew up. And before dropping off to sleep, I quickly hardened myself to the idea that, for me, there could be no cosy, childhood retreat, in which I could really rest; and that if, on account of it, I happened to be limited, then it must be solely from within myself that I would have to make my way forward into time; and that the bare room in which I was lying could easily serve for me as a symbol of whatever story lay ahead: as if it might be the blank of some unwritten page that is simply waiting to be filled, and needing only the swift movement of a pen, in order to bear its action forward.

The next morning, almost immediately after breakfast, I spoke to Mr Carson and told him of my decision. I couldn't quite tell whether he was pleased about it or not; but thought that this was probably due to the fact that he had been taught by his experience not to reveal himself in such matters. All he said was, 'If you do run into trouble, Richard – if you feel confused, I mean, or in any way upset, you will contact me, won't you? Just give me a ring and I'll do my best to help . . . I would also be interested to know what happens,' he added; 'whether you actually meet your father or not – or whatever. I think you can appreciate that I'm bound to be curious about it; and besides which, I am fond of you, as I think you know; and Mrs Carson is too. We've seen you grow from a boy into a young man, so our interest in you is a natural one.'

I thanked him for what he had said, and promised to do what he had asked; and even shook hands with him, in a rather formal way; almost as if we had just signed some legal agreement – which I noticed he seemed to be thankful for; and which, because it gave shape and order to our exchange, prevented us from having to cope too directly with our emotions, which I think was a problem for us both.

'Now. What are you going to do with yourself before lunch?' Mr Carson asked. 'The town's lively on a Saturday, what with the market. In any case, lunch is at one, Richard. Sharp – as always: so do please be back before then. I don't know what it will be, I'm afraid. Shepherd's pie, probably – that's a usual dish on a Saturday. But with it being so cold, you won't say no to that, I expect'; and in which, of course, he was right.

I'd not been into the town for a very long time indeed. Often during my stays, I would avoid it altogether; partly because all my schoolfriends had moved away from the area; and also because what I enjoyed more was to go for a long stroll in the countryside, where I knew I could be alone. However, for some reason – perhaps because of the cold – I chose to follow Mr Carson's suggestion; and after wrapping myself up warmly, went for a brisk walk into the town, where I enjoyed the busyness of the small market-square, that was tightly packed with stalls selling fruit, vegetables, clothing, coconut-matting, secondhand bric-a-brac and so forth; and where I was attracted (I don't know why) by a crowd of people that had gathered before an enormous butcher's van; one whole side of which had been opened up to the square and propped up to form an awning; and inside of which, set on a platform high above the crowd; and behind a long, wooden counter that ran the entire length of the van; a row of hearty-looking butchers were carving cheap, rough cuts of meat; then weighing each cut with quantities of various kinds of offal and stuffing it all into a bag: then taking bids for it from the crowd below; and then, as soon as a price had been agreed upon, throwing the bag into a steep, zinc-lined chute and allowing it to tumble down to a black-haired woman in a stiff white apron; who, in exchange for the agreed sum of money, then handed it to the buyer.

It was a curiously medieval sight, and slightly revolting, I found, with all the lurid reds and pinks of the meat blending with the darker colour of the offal – of liver and kidney, I mean – and with the pale, yellowish tissues of the tripe, heavily stained by blood.

I can hardly say that I enjoyed it; but because I had been drawn to it, I felt there must be a certain harshness about it that I needed to be aware of at that moment; with all the hard-faced country people in their thick winter clothing; and the fierce, bawdy cries of the butchers, as they excited the crowd to this buy or that; making a kind of show of it by dipping a hand beneath the counter to draw out a gigantic string of sausages; then chopping off a few and adding them to the rest of the bargain: then laughing and making a lewd joke of it; shouting at the men in the crowd, "Ere, mister! These'll be for the missus!'

When I left the market-square and began my walk back to the house, it had just turned a quarter past twelve; and because it was only a mile away, I knew that I would be in plenty of time for lunch. And as so often happens at the end of February, the weather had slipped back to the lower temperatures of early January; and a huge blanket of dull, pinkish-grey cloud seemed to threaten a sudden fall of snow. So I hurried along, cutting through the small side streets of the town to the main roadway, that led directly to the north, and that I had walked so many times as a boy; knowing each twist and turn of it, and knowing as well that, after a while, the house would appear between the hedgerows, set on a rise towards the left.

I passed no-one. A bullock, standing behind the wooden bars of a gate, stamped its forefeet as I went by, and let out a sharp, noisy snort of breath that froze almost immediately, and seemed to hover in the air; and farther along the road, two enormous black crows swooped down from the tangled branches of an old oak tree, to strut before me in their velvet-feathered suits: then, as they spread their wings, and as they again rose slowly into the air, let out a raucous, sinister cry that echoed across the countryside. And somehow, the sight and sound of them, combined with those of the blood-stained butchers in the market-place, seemed to unnerve me. Instead of feeling happy, as I had expected to feel, and as I had certainly felt earlier, when I had left the house, I now felt almost the opposite; and it made me anxious to be indoors again.

Looking back at that moment, I cannot help wondering whether all of our life – or certainly a great deal more of it than we think – isn't really subjective; and that, by some means or another, we are all linked through our psyches to some great network of inner rhythms and actions, of which we are only partially aware; but which – nonetheless, is affecting us continually.

I say this, because I had a distinct feeling of danger just then; and as I walked briskly along, my heart began to beat more quickly, and my breathing became shorter and more rapid. My rational mind told me that what I was feeling made no sense: that I could have seen that butcher's van on any Saturday of the year; and that the mere squawking of two black crows, was something with which anyone who had lived in the country as I had done, must be familiar. But inside me, at a much deeper level, it seemed that some area of my brain had been responding to messages passed through my body that went against such rational thought. It was as if a series of warning bells had been sounded, telling me that something must be amiss. I wasn't able to think about this directly, of course. It was impossible for me then to be at all objective about what I was feeling. Yet I had an instinctive knowledge that something must be wrong, or must have happened – and because of that, my eyes searched anxiously beyond each new turning in the road; knowing as they did that the house must soon come into view; and thinking that once I had reached its safety, the danger would be expelled; and that the cause of what I was feeling would turn out to be some mere temporary bout of nervousness – to do, perhaps, with my having drifted briefly into the past; and perhaps as well, with my being so keen to return to London, where I would make that appointment with the solicitor, and so take the first step towards my father.

Eventually, as I turned a sharp corner in the road – and as I passed the bulky form of a dark holly bush, that loomed out menacingly from the hedgerow – I caught a glimpse of the house; standing on a steady rise of ground; with its short driveway leading up to its sturdy, half-columned entrance. And as I did so, I noticed a figure standing in the partly opened doorway. I couldn't recognise who it was. All I could see was that the person was wearing a uniform, and was obviously a female member of the staff; and that she appeared to be anxiously scanning the driveway, as if she was expecting someone to arrive.

As I quickened my steps, I saw the person turn and go inside; and then, because I was now so much closer to the house, I was able to recognise the figure of Mr Carson, who also appeared at the doorway, and who began to look in the same direction.

For some reason, I felt that I should call out to him, but feared that my doing so might make me appear silly. However, no sooner had I left the road, and turned into the driveway of the house than he caught sight of me. And as he too turned to go inside, he waved his hands vigorously at me, as if he was urging me to hurry.

Needless to say, my heart was now beating even more rapidly than before, and I broke into a quick trot; then sprinted up the steps into the entrance-hall, where I more or less collided with Mr Carson, who had just come out of his study.

'Oh, Richard,' he said, 'I was looking for you. There's a call for you from London. Something urgent.'

'For me?' I asked, finding it difficult to believe, since I had left my address with no-one.

'Yes. I said you were expected back at any moment and they asked to hang on. It's not a minute since they rang. Take it in my study. It's someone called –'

I didn't wait to hear the name. Driven forward by the apprehension I had been feeling, I simply muttered a brief thankyou to Mr Carson, and rushed quickly to the phone.

'Hello,' I said, half out of breath, 'this is Richard – Richard Constable.'

'Richard. It's George.'

'George?' My mind repeated the name several times, before I could make out who it really was.

'George?' I asked aloud.

'Yes. You're out of breath.'

'I've just come in. I'd been for a walk. Sorry,' I said.

'Richard, it's about Chuck. He's had an accident.'

My brain couldn't gear itself to this, and I had to ask him to repeat what he had just said.

'An accident – yes. On his bike. He asked Darby to contact me at the hostel to see if I knew your number.'

'Which you didn't,' I answered, not really thinking of what I was saying, but using it to gain time.

'No – but I remembered the name of the town: knew it to be in Berkshire – and found the number of the "home" through Enquiries. . . . And I asked to speak to Mr Carson. I remembered his name from the letter.'

'Oh,' I said, still unable to respond.

'It happened last night,' George continued, ' – late. Darby rang me about an hour ago.'

'An accident George?' I asked, taking in the news at last.

'Yes.'

'Serious, you mean?'

'Yes.'

'Oh.'

'He's in St George's. Darby said that he was anxious that you should know.'

'Oh,' I repeated, unable to think of what to say: then, pulling myself together, asked how serious it really was.

'I don't know,' said George. 'Darby just said serious – that's all. To be honest, I was half asleep when he rang.'

'St George's, you say?'

'Yes.'

'Have you seen him?'

'No, of course I haven't. Darby rang just an hour ago, as I just said. But I'll go there today, if you'd like me to. If you've a message, I mean; and if he's seeable, of course.'

'George,' I said, my mind suddenly focusing itself, 'If I come back today. If I come back this afternoon, could you meet me, do you think?'

'Today?' he asked, sounding a little surprised. 'At what time?'

I told him that I didn't know, but would ring him back; and after he had given me his number – which I realised I half knew by heart; because I had used it so often, of course, when I had lived at the hostel myself – I hurried to find Mr and Mrs Carson, in order to tell them what had happened: explaining to them that Chuck shared the flat with me in South Kensington, and that the accident appeared to be serious.

'Do you want to go back today, Richard?' asked Mrs Carson, before I had time to speak my thoughts. 'I think you would like to; and I think that you should.'

I asked for the time of a train from Reading; and Mr Carson insisted upon taking me there by car. 'We'll go as soon as we can,' he said. 'Emma, do please see if we can have lunch immediately. We'll go as soon as we can, Richard,' he repeated to me. 'After lunch. Immediately.'

Mrs Carson hurried off with an anxious look on her face, and as soon as Mr Carson had given me the time of the train, I rang George back at the hostel, and my meeting with him was settled.

'Now,' said Mr Carson, as we went to table, 'We'll have a good hot lunch: and you'll do your best to eat it, Richard. A full stomach is a settler. You'll feel steadier for it . . . It's not shepherd's pie,' he added, as we sat down. 'It's steak and kidney pud. Now, what could be better than that?'

There was no talk of literature at that meal: none of Mrs Carson's quick chatter. Both of them were as concerned about things as I was; asking me questions about Chuck: about how old he was; whether he had parents: how long I had known him: whether I was very fond of him; and saying how upsetting it was bound to be for me, but that it might be less serious than I imagined. And saying too that it was thoughtful of Chuck to have let me know; and good of whoever it was that had telephoned, and had given me the message.

I answered as best I could: spoke a little about Chuck, and a little about George; and did what I could to eat some lunch. But what I was really preoccupied with just then was how much Chuck seemed to mean to me; and also how glad I would be once I had caught the train, and once I was on my way to London.

# X

YOU ARE PROBABLY anticipating that the opening sequence of this chapter is to be my arrival at Paddington station, with George waiting to meet me, and with us going off together to see Chuck. And to be quite frank with you, I had been thinking along those lines myself. However, I feel that I must first relate to you something that is totally out of sequence. You will judge this unfair of me, perhaps; and might say, perhaps, that, by doing this, I shall be spoiling your pleasure in the story. But as I have put it to you before, it seems to me that for a tale to be told properly it doesn't necessarily have to proceed in a purely linear way – in the sense, I mean, of a 'then he did this, then he did that' sort of thing; because, of course, the danger of that too simple kind of storytelling isn't just that it can prove boring, it can also cause the reader – and the storyteller too, for that matter – to lose touch with the true centre of the book; and if this should occur, then the reader can feel cheated – as if he or she had been caught out by a too obvious form of chronology. All good tales have to have their diversions, since it's the story's journey that counts as experience; and the last thing I would wish for, would be to cause you to kind of tumble out of the book at the end, so to speak; simply because I have pressed too hard towards its conclusion.

That, at any rate, is what I guess to be my reason for now telling you something that occurred almost two weeks after my return from the country; and once I've done that, I'll go back to my arrival at Paddington station, on that afternoon in late February, and after Mr Carson had kindly put me on the train at Reading.

Actually – to be more specific about it – there are two things I feel a need to speak about. They aren't faults or errors, thank goodness, but one concerns something I said about Chuck at the very beginning of the book; about his being more of a mum to me than a dad, and about this being the reason why we eventually had to part. And the other has to do with George; which I feel a need to have over and done with; and which is something so astonishing – or it was to me, at least – that I'd rather get that out of the way, before pressing on with what will be the closing chapters of my tale; which have to do with my visiting Chuck in hospital – and, shortly after that, with my making a first contact with the solicitor to find out more about my father.

First then, about Chuck. As Mr and Mrs Carson had said might be the case, his accident turned out to be a less serious one than I had imagined. He had cracked two bones in his right arm, was badly bruised down the same side of his body, and had gashed his forehead and suffered some slight concussion as well. But it was nothing too deeply serious and his stay in hospital proved comparatively brief, in that he was discharged in a little over a week, and allowed to come home to rest and recuperate.

I had begged him to go either to his parents, both of whom I had met briefly at the hospital (as you are later going to find out); or to ask Jack if he could possibly stay for a while at his aunt's – at Bognor; where I felt that Jack and Bridget would take good care of him.

But he would have none of that. What he wanted was to come home to the flat; and he was sure that he – or rather that *we* – could manage. There was no way in which I could deny him this; and I must admit that he did make it sound reasonable; passing off his injuries as slight, and saying that it would be a mere day or two before he'd be off on his bike again, and back to work in the City.

But I had my doubts about it being the right thing to do, and felt instinctively that it might put too much strain upon our relationship. Chuck wasn't an easy person to live with, as you well know; and to have to cope with him when his body was out of order I felt certain would be difficult.

I prepared for his return with a considerable amount of care: making sure, for instance, that I had bought in the list of things he had given me in the hospital – things like food, I mean, washing powders and the like: had given the flat a good clean (something I hadn't bothered with when he was away); and had even taken a couple of days off from work, so that I could help him to settle in more easily.

It had been arranged at the hospital that an ambulance

would bring him home and that I would wait for him to arrive – and then, if necessary, would give him some help in climbing the stairs. 'I'm not being carried up on a bloody stretcher, Bo,' he had said to me, when I had been to see him the night before. 'It's not as if I'm some bloody invalid.'

At about ten-thirty in the morning, I heard the ambulance draw up in the street below: heard Chuck say something to the ambulance men about being able to manage the stairs on his own; and as soon as I heard him enter the main hallway of the building, I went out on to the landing to see if he needed help.

'Is that you, Chuck?' I more or less shouted, to assure him that I was there.

'No,' his voice came echoing up the stairway, 'it's the fucking Queen of Sheba.'

I hated it when Chuck spoke in that manner in public – which was how I thought of the staircase, since several flats were served by it, and I could imagine that one of our neighbours might hear.

'Shall I come down,' I called out, 'or can you manage?'

'No,' he answered again – still very loud. 'You stay where you are, Bo. I'm going to see if I can do it by myself.'

I waited patiently, hearing his slow, heavy tread, as he gradually made his way up. Then, as he at last came into view, turning on to the landing immediately beneath me, he paused to catch his breath.

His head was still swathed in bandages and his arm was now in a sling; and for some reason – perhaps due to the general shock that his system had suffered – he looked as if he had been in a nasty fight, and as if he had been bruised and battered all over.

'It's the bloody Invisible Man,' he said to me with a grim laugh, as he waited to mount the final brief flight of stairs. 'Did you ever see it, Bo? Claude Rains, it was. Bloody marvellous.'

The sight of him had quite startled me. For one thing, he suddenly looked and seemed so old. I had the impression that I was encountering some well-built elderly gentleman, who had been forced to pause out of a more natural necessity: due to his age, I mean, rather than to his having suffered a recent accident.

'No, I didn't,' I replied (meaning *The Invisible Man*, of course). 'I've heard about it, though. He had to be wrapped in bandages to be seen. Is that what it was?'

'Yes – that's it,' Chuck answered, as he clutched the banister with his left hand; and as he began to make his slow ascent to our landing. 'Never thought I'd be that: the fucking Invisible Man.'

I was relieved to hear that he could find some humour in it all, because it really pained me to see him in such a restricted condition. It made me so conscious of how the free exuberance of his physique was such an important part of his make-up; and of how dependent he seemed to be upon it for his bouncy system of defence.

'You sure you can manage, Chuck?' I asked him.

'Yes, I'll manage,' he answered, in a gruff tone of voice. 'You stay there, Bo. I'll make it. I didn't want those bastards who brought me back to be carrying me up in a chair or something; or on a stretcher. I hope you've got some booze in, 'cos that's what I need. No wonder they kill people off in hospital, allowing no bloody drink in the wards.'

I watched him as he pulled himself on to the final step; then went forward to help him into the flat, thinking that he had made his point and had achieved his aim. But he half pushed me away with a crude thrust of his body.

'I told you. I don't need your *help*, Bo,' he repeated. 'Now; stand back from the door, for Christ's sake. The difficulty is going to be to cross from the banister to the doorway.'

I did as he had asked; and stood well away from the entrance, as he paused to estimate the distance, and the energy needed to cross it. Then he suddenly lurched across the landing and more or less stumbled into the flat.

'There now,' he said, as he collapsed into the armchair in my room, and as he looked at me from beneath his bandages with his huge, sorrowful eyes, 'I've made it. That's what I've done. I've fucking well made it . . . Just get my bag, Bo – will you? – it's in the hall.'

Chuck slept for most of the afternoon, and the evening passed off quietly; interrupted only by a brief telephone-call from his parents and one from his friend Darby, asking if he was all right. I can't say that he was ever cheerful, and there was no sign of that bouncy, humorous defence of his; but he wasn't miserable either, and was quite decent about my having to get the supper; giving me instructions regarding it, it's true, but not being *all* that bossy or difficult; and we decided between us that it would be best if we both got to bed early. He had had a stiff drink, soon after he had arrived at the flat in the morning, but he didn't ask for another; and I avoided drinking myself, out of a fear that he might be tempted by my example.

I wanted to help him to undress, because it was obvious that he had little use of his right arm – and was still in some pain I thought as well; but he insisted that he could manage, and even thanked me for making the offer; and as I settled down for the night, I was relieved to hear him hum a brief tune or two; almost as if he was singing himself to sleep.

However, the following day proved a different matter. I had purposefully taken it off, as you already know; and after that peaceful evening together, I was now looking forward to it: so much so, in fact, that I couldn't help wondering why it was that I should be so fearful about him at times.

Shortly after ten that morning our doorbell rang. It was Molly – Chuck's cousin; asking how Chuck was and wanting to see him.

'Who is it, Bo?' his voice bellowed from his room.

'It's Molly, Chuck.'

'Who?'

'Molly. Your cousin.'

'Tell her to piss off.'

I felt embarrassed by this and stood back to let Molly in; noticing that she hadn't cringed at all when Chuck had been so rude to her, and seemed almost impervious to his savage type of expression.

'Chuck – are you decent?' she called out, as she paused in the small entrance-hall.

'I thought I told you to piss off,' he answered, as Molly appeared in his doorway.

'Piss off yourself,' his cousin retorted with a quick laugh. 'I've not come to see you, you fat lump. I've come to see Richard.'

' 'Course you have,' replied Chuck. 'You don't need to tell us that. I've warned him about you, you know. If it's money you're after, he hasn't got any; and neither have I.'

'My God,' said Molly, ignoring this, 'You do look a sight, Chuck – doesn't he, Richard? I hadn't expected him to be all bandaged up.'

'I'm the fucking Invisible Man – that's what I am,' Chuck threw back at her. 'Now, get out of my room, so that I can dress . . . Richard'll give you a cup of coffee if you behave yourself.'

Molly turned to smile at me; and in such a warm and affectionate manner I thought, that I couldn't help smiling at her in return; and I nodded to her to join me in the kitchen, as Chuck hobbled across his room and closed the door.

'How's it been, Rich?' she asked, abbreviating my name.

'He shouldn't be here, you know. He ought to have gone to his parents; or to Dodo's. She thinks the world of him. She'd have been glad to have him at Bognor. It wasn't your place to have to cope with him on your own.'

I assured her that as yet he had been no trouble, and that I was glad to be able to help. 'He's not *all* that difficult,' I remember saying. 'It seems to depend on – well, I don't know; almost on the weather, I think. Anyway, as yet he's been more than well behaved. Last night, for instance, he even thanked me; and that's something I don't remember him doing before.'

'Well, I just hope for your sake that it stays that way,' said Molly, offering me a cigarette, and as we sat down to drink our coffee. 'If it doesn't, you will get in touch with me – won't you, Richard? Here's my number,' she said, fishing a card out of her handbag. 'Just give me a ring and I'll speak to his parents or something.'

I thanked her, and felt that behind her offer there was genuine concern: that she knew Chuck only too well; and that being a little like him, perhaps, she was aware of how turbulent he could be on occasions. Perhaps too, she sensed some kind of animal danger in him; because I can recall thinking to myself how there was something almost circus-like about her personality; and that this wasn't provoked at all by the knowledge I had that she practised the art of juggling. It was more because I could so easily picture her in a circus-ring; dressed as a lion-tamer, I thought.

'Doesn't it bother you,' I asked, 'when Chuck speaks to you as he did just now?'

'How do you mean?'

'Well, when he was rude to you.'

'Oh, that. No – of course not. He's always been like that. I'm used to it. Besides, I've learned to answer him back.'

As Molly said this, Chuck made his way into the kitchen and slumped into a chair beside us at the table.

'So what are you two mumbling on about?' he asked, as he stared at us with his enormous, clownlike eyes.

'We were talking about *you*,' Molly answered quickly. 'Richard says you're being good; says you're behaving yourself.'

'Like fuck I am,' he said with a scowl. 'Where's the whisky, Richard? Aren't you going to offer us a drink? She's a right one for the bottle, is our Molly,' he said, with a nod towards his cousin. 'Eh? Aren't you, Moll . . . ? Likes a drop of the old tiddly.'

I asked Molly if she'd care for a drink, rather hoping that she'd say no; but I guess that Chuck was right about her being a drinker, because she quickly threw back her head, pushed one of her fat, dumpy little hands through her short, curly gold locks; then let out a swift puff of smoke and said, 'Love one.'

'And you, Chuck?' I asked, hoping with all my heart that he would refuse.

'Me?' he answered with a leer, 'I want a big one – like *that*,' indicating with his fingers what I could only picture would be a tumbler full. 'And *you're* having one too,' he added, in what I thought was a threatening way.

'Not in the morning, Chuck,' I said to him quickly. 'I never drink during the day, and you know it.'

'Oh – is that *so*?' he threw back at me.

'Yes, it *is*,' I answered firmly, as I went to fetch the whisky – and as I then cleverly added the suggestion that, since he had his cousin to keep him company, I'd use it to take a brief walk; and perhaps to buy a few things at the grocer's.

'Fucking coward,' he said, as I passed him and went to my room. 'You're a shit, Richard!' he called out, 'that's what you are – isn't he, Moll?'

I didn't wait to hear Molly's reply. I was only too pleased to have made my escape, from what I feared might become one of Chuck's big scenes. And as soon as I had slipped into my donkey-jacket, I ran swiftly down to the street, slamming the door of the flat behind me.

It was a lovely day. The low winter sunlight was cutting through the narrow side streets and alleyways and casting sharp beams of light upon the traffic. There was a distinct feeling of spring being in the air; and that, after what had been a difficult winter, the weather was about to make its first brave move towards summer, and seemed full of promises, as a result.

I determined to make the most of Molly's visit, and set out for a good walk; making my way along the Cromwell Road towards the west, then turning down towards the Brompton Road and circling back to South Kensington. I did enjoy it; and by the time I had bought the few things we needed at the grocer's, had quite forgotten about Chuck, and about my having left him and Molly with the whisky bottle.

However, as I opened the entrance-door of our building I heard what I thought was a scream; then the noise of someone rushing down the stairs – and then, as I turned on to the first landing, saw that it was Molly.

'Don't go in there, Richard!' she shrieked at me. 'Stay away from him!' – and with that, she dashed past me and down to the floor below. I wasn't quite sure whether I had imagined it or not, but I had the impression that she had wrapped one of her hands in a handkerchief; and although there were no signs of any blood, for some reason pictured that she had injured herself.

'Molly!' I called out to her, as I heard her pull open the entrance-door of the building. 'Molly!' I repeated – but it was too late. I heard the door closing itself behind her and knew that she was already out of hearing, and that there was no means of my knowing what had happened; or why it was that she had shrieked such a savage warning.

Had Chuck attacked her? That was the first thought that came to my head; or had he just been difficult and abusive; and she perhaps knocked herself, as she got up to get away? And should I heed her warning? I asked myself; or should I think, as I was half inclined to do, that she was simply being hysterical (since, from the way she had pushed back her hair and said, 'Love one,' when I had asked her about the whisky, I had already come to the conclusion that she might have a tendency to be that.)

I had a paper carrier-bag in my hand – there were few plastic ones in those days – with fresh bread in it and milk; and for some reason, I just couldn't see myself turning back, and taking it out with me into the street again. And in any case, I had nowhere to go; unless I went to the pub, perhaps, which I guessed would now be open. But somehow that also didn't make sense, since, as I have said, I never drank during the day. So there seemed to be no choice for me but to go up and into the flat, and to see exactly what had happened. If I took my time – if I went slowly, I told myself, Chuck would probably have calmed down; and perhaps too, I thought, I should give him some warning that I was returning.

The door of the flat had been left slightly ajar, so I carefully pushed it open. 'Chuck?' I called out quietly, as I stepped into the hallway.

There was no reply – and the first thing that struck me was how dark the flat appeared to be. In the kitchen to my right, a thick green blind – one that we seldom used – had been pulled down to block out the light; and ahead of me, I could see that the curtains in my room had been drawn; allowing only one narrow ribbon of sunlight to cut fiercely across my bed, and to streak its way up to the ceiling. And so intense was this light that I found it difficult to see into the shadows that surrounded it.

'Chuck?' I repeated, as I then turned towards the left, and went towards his room.

Again there was no reply, and I saw that his room was even darker than my own. Had he gone out, I wondered; or had he perhaps locked himself in the bathroom?

Cautiously, I tested its door with my hand; and it at once swung open under the pressure. But there was no-one inside. Things there were neat and orderly and no blind had been drawn – and it was then that I thought of the lavatory, and guessed that he must be there.

'Chuck,' I called out. 'Are you all right?'

Yet again there was no reply; but when I placed an ear to the door, I could hear the sound of his heavy breathing.

'Chuck,' I said, 'what's wrong. Are you all right?'

'Piss off,' came the dark, sullen reply.

I thought it would be wisest to retreat and to leave him alone; knowing that so often when I did that, he would quickly recover his balance. And knowing too that, although he would never apologise for what he had done, or for any upset he might have caused, he would quickly be behaving as if nothing unusual had happened.

I took the milk and bread into the kitchen and released the blind: then went into my room with the intention of drawing back the curtains. But as I did so, I noticed that my bedclothes had been pulled back, and that a heavy kitchen-knife had been plunged into my pillow: also, that the small cupboard by my bed had been ransacked, and that one of my letters had been savagely torn into shreds, which were scattered about the floor.

I picked up a few fragments of the letter – and, turning them over, saw quickly that it was the one George had sent me from Scotland, and that Chuck had opened without my permission. And the combination unnerved me – the sight of the torn letter; and of the knife plunged into my pillow.

Perhaps Molly had been right, I told myself. Perhaps Chuck really is dangerous. Perhaps I should gather some of my things together and escape. The atmosphere seemed so menacing, I was glad I hadn't closed the door of the flat when I came in; and I immediately felt less threatened once I had rushed across to the window and had pushed its curtains aside.

Something told me that I must keep my nerve: that at all costs I should show no sign of panic: that I should remove the knife from the pillow: that I should take it back into the kitchen: that I should gather up the shredded fragments of the letter; and place them with all the other papers in the drawer. And I mustn't hurry, I told myself. I must act steadily and deliberately, and create an aura of behaving normally, as if I was simply tidying my room. If possible, I said to myself, I should hum a tune; or even whistle one, perhaps.

I was able to do neither, alas, but I did manage to carry out the two actions that I had planned; and although my pillow had been pierced, and there were a few of its feathers lying about, I was able to calmly turn it over, and draw the bedclothes up to cover it.

But as I did this, I became conscious of the fact that my mind was also taking the decision that this must be the dividing line: that, however fond I might be of Chuck – and even in that heightened moment of near terror, I knew that I would in some way always feel close to him – my life with him in the flat couldn't possibly continue. I had no conception of where I would go, unless I went back to the hostel, perhaps (which I would dislike doing intensely). But I knew for certain that by the time that day had ended I would have left.

Once I had put things in order, I sat down in the armchair by my bed and took out a cigarette, doing my utmost to remain calm. How long I sat there I really don't know; but I must have smoked at least two more cigarettes before I heard the slow flush of the lavatory cistern, and before Chuck appeared in my doorway.

To show that I was ready to confront him, I stood up. And as had so often happened in the past, he quickly turned away; lowering both his head and his eyes, and appearing to be sorry for himself.

He was a pathetic sight – even a tragic one, I thought – with his dishevelled hair, and his wounded arm half dangling out of its sling; and with the fingers of his left hand still fumbling clumsily with his fly-buttons.

'I warned you, Bo – didn't I?' he muttered, in a low, heavy tone of voice.

'About what?' I answered sharply.

'About that piss-arse George,' he said, throwing me a quick furtive glance from beneath his lowered eyebrows.

'About George?' I asked. 'What about George?'

'You shouldn't have had him here, Bo – that's what I mean. You should have got rid of him.'

'Had him *here*?' I blurted back at him.

'He slept here – didn't he? – when I was in hospital.'

Suddenly I realised what he had been imagining.

'Look, Chuck,' I said, speaking the truth – and it really *was* the truth, 'I've not seen George – I've not even *heard* from him since I came back from Berkshire, ten days ago: since he met me at the station; and since he came with me to the hospital.'

Chuck looked at me in amazement.

'That's the truth,' I said, 'and you'd better believe it. Now, I'm going to telephone your parents and ask them if you can go there for a few days. We can't go on like this,

Chuck. I did wrong to give you the whisky. I don't know what happened between you and Molly and I don't want to know; but what I *do* know is that I can't go back to work tomorrow and leave you here like this. It's all *wrong*. So I'm ringing your parents and you're going there. You understand that – don't you?'

I think he couldn't quite believe that I was saying this; and as I passed him to go to the phone, he turned to stare at me; almost as if he was daring me to continue. But he put up no real resistance; and must have realised, I think, that he had gone too far, and that I had made up my mind to leave. I don't think he sensed that I would be doing it that very evening; but I did seem to know that somewhere, at the very back of his mind, he was half conscious of the fact that the life we shared in the flat was about to come to an end; and that it was now beyond his power to repair things.

His parents, I am glad to say, were more than ready to have him, and were upset to know that he had caused me so much trouble. And although they lived on the very outskirts of the city – towards Hertfordshire – Chuck's father assured me that he would come to collect him a little later in the day – or shortly after teatime, as he put it; which I must admit worried me somewhat, since I would have been happier if he had come to collect him immediately; and if Chuck could have left in less than an hour. But I quickly told myself that I would need to pack Chuck's things for him, and that this would occupy me for a while; and I would also encourage Chuck to have a bath, I thought, since he looked so jaded and unwell, and so unhealthy-looking in general.

'Your father will be here at five,' I said, giving some definition to the time, 'so I'm going to get your things packed and you're having a bath. Just tell me what you want to take with you, and I'll pack it into a suitcase.'

I had never behaved with Chuck in this fashion before;

and was astonished to learn that it worked so well; and that he became so docile and obedient.

'Do I keep my sling on, Bo?' he asked, as I began to run his bath water.

Not once did I allow my energy to slacken. Relentlessly, I pushed through the afternoon, popping in and out of the bathroom; asking him if he wanted to take this or that, and then packing it with care.

There was one dangerous moment, when he was attempting to dry himself, and he asked me to rub his back; because he took the chance it offered to grab me with his left arm; and in a teasing way, attempted to draw me towards his wet body. But I had skill enough to handle it; and by the time he was dressed, and by the time I had made him some tea and some buttered toast, a kind of jollity of the spirit had begun to return to us both – akin to the type I had so often experienced on a Sunday, when we were doing our weekly chores.

'You're a cunning little bastard, Bo,' he said to me, as the daylight began to fade. 'You're getting rid of me – aren't you?'

'I am not getting *rid* of you, Chuck,' I asserted. 'You just can't be left here alone all day. That's all there is to it. Now – finish your tea, will you? Your father will be here at any moment.'

The next few minutes proved the most difficult ones. The humour between us subsided and we became at a loss for words. So I went to collect his suitcase from his room and carried it into the entrance-hall; then returned to collect his overcoat and scarf, hoping that by the time I had done this, the doorbell would have sounded and Chuck would be on his way. But it didn't turn out like that, and I was forced to return to the kitchen and to confront Chuck yet again.

'I'll miss you, Bo,' he said to me in a very simple way, and for once looking directly into my eyes.

'We'll miss each other,' I answered curtly, 'that's the truth of it . . . Look, Chuck, let me help you on with your overcoat . . . Your father said to me on the phone that he didn't want to hang about once he was here; because he feared becoming caught up in the evening traffic.'

And to my relief, he did what I had asked; and by the time he had put on his scarf and then his coat, and I had carefully buttoned the latter over the arm that was in a sling, the doorbell finally rang and Chuck was on his way – with no complaints or grumbles; no heavy, maudlin expressions of sentiment: just one short burst of his bouncy laughter as his father went down the stairs ahead of him, and as he turned to pinch my cheek and to whisper into my ear, 'Remember, Bo – be careful with your willie'; which was a typical phrase for him as you know; and in a certain sense, one that brought our relationship fittingly to a close.

I shall always see him as he turned on to the landing below, and as he raised his left hand to me in salute; because I really do believe that for all his occasional violence – and what I suppose I must call the near-madness in him as well – he is one of the richest people I have known, and also one of the bravest. And he had been perfectly right about George, since what I had said to Chuck had been true – concerning which, you are now to learn more, when you read the following chapter.

# XI

AS YOU ALREADY know, after he had rung me about Chuck's accident, George was there at the station to meet me when the train pulled in from Reading. I had been sitting at the front of the train, close to the engine; and as it drew slowly in at the platform, I could see him standing beyond the ticket-barrier, surrounded by a smallish gathering of Londoners, whose watchful, eager expressions showed that they were waiting for their loved ones.

He didn't see me, however, until I was handing in my ticket; then strode forward to shake my hand in what I certainly took to be a friendly enough manner. But there was something about him, I thought – maybe a curious look in his eye – that made him seem to be different.

'Thanks for meeting me,' I said.

'Oh, it's nothing,' he answered, as if it really was. 'How was the journey?'

Because it was the last thing I had on my mind, I didn't quite know how to respond to this; so I just said, 'Oh, fine, I guess, though I don't remember it much. I was worrying about Chuck.'

George said nothing; and (in order to make conversation, I suppose) I asked if there was further news of Chuck.

'No,' he said twice, as we began to make our way out of the station, 'not since Darby rang.'

'Oh,' I replied, allowing that matter to drop; and then, although I assumed it to be his intention, I asked him if he was coming with me to the hospital to see Chuck. But he didn't respond to this either; and simply said that we'd be taking a bus to Marble Arch, and then perhaps another to Hyde Park Corner; or we could walk along Park Lane.

As usual, I put myself into his hands, believing that he had thought things out, and that what he had decided would be for the best; but once we had climbed on to the bus, I noticed that his behaviour suddenly changed, and instead of being his normal, confident self, he appeared anxious.

'George?' I asked, as if he knew everything, 'is Chuck going to die?'

'Goodness me, no,' he said, as he tapped the empty bowl of his pipe against the back of the seat in front of him, 'Darby said serious – but not more: not life and death, I mean.'

'Oh,' I answered a second time, taking this in; and then, because it was something I would think about occasionally, I asked him if he had ever seen anyone die.

'Die? – no,' he answered, sucking his pipe, 'but I've seen a dead body, if that's what you mean.'

I told him that I hadn't been meaning that; and didn't think I was keen to see either.

'Well, you're going to at some time or another – that's for sure,' he said with a hard expression on his face. 'I saw my grandfather's body, and I can't say that I exactly liked it. I was just twelve at the time, and I remember how my father made me kiss him.'

I didn't tell George how much I disliked not having a grandfather, and how strongly it affected me, when anyone spoke to me as he had just done – about family matters, I mean: not thinking, of course, how unlike me they were in that respect; but I recall how strongly that image then fixed itself in my mind; and how foreign it seemed to me that George should have not only a father, but a grandfather as well; and that one of them should have forced him to kiss the other.

We decided not to walk the second part of our journey, but to take a bus to Hyde Park Corner that would more or less deposit us at the hospital; and as soon as we were on it,

George said to me, 'If you don't mind, Richard, I won't go in with you to see Chuck. It's not that I don't want to see him. It's just that I've already made an appointment for this evening, to see a friend of mine at college; and I can't put it off. We're meeting at Piccadilly – at six, and there's no time . . . You don't mind – do you?' he half repeated, looking at me out of the corner of his eye. 'I didn't know this was going to happen, and that you would be coming back today.'

I felt terribly unhappy when George said this. It was selfish and unthinking of me, I suppose, to have assumed that he would be free, and that he would be keeping me company for the evening; and if I'm to be honest, I had half pictured how we'd have the flat to ourselves for once, and that this would be something that he would welcome. However, I didn't express my unhappiness, and just mumbled something about Chuck being disappointed – which wouldn't be true, of course – and that I could more than understand. And I felt relieved when he said that he would ring me the following day. Or, at least, that is what I convinced myself he had said: though what his actual words had been were, 'I'll probably ring you tomorrow,' which isn't quite the same thing.

None the less, it was enough to make me feel comfortable; and as we began to approach the entrance of the hospital, allowed me to concentrate upon Chuck rather than upon George. In fact, when George turned to leave it enabled me to behave cheerfully, as I remember; and to even say thank you to him a second time for having met me at the station.

'I'll give your regards to Chuck,' I called out as he left; to which he had answered with a curt nod of his head; and then, as he strode quickly off out of sight, I turned to enter the hospital, wondering what it would be like, since I'd not been inside such a building before; and also how I would discover where Chuck was, in what seemed such an impressive institution; and wondering too whether he would be well enough to see me or even to recognise me; and whether or not he would be surrounded by a host of other invalid figures, all swathed in bandages and things, and smelling of ether, I thought; and whether I ought to have brought him grapes or something – or a book, perhaps; neither of which I had thought of until that moment.

Finding Chuck proved the easiest thing in the world; since a receptionist at a desk close to the entrance told me that, although he might be moved from there in a day or two, he had been put into a room, rather than a ward; and gave me instructions as to where I should go: which of the staircases I must use and which of the various corridors I must follow.

'Room twenty-three,' she had told me with a smile; and – after following her directions with some care – that number appeared on a door ahead of me.

Approaching it, I could hear voices, and saw that the door was partly ajar. Then, as I was stepping forward to go in, a nurse appeared beside me in the corridor, carrying a small, enamelled tray, upon which there seemed to be a number of surgical instruments.

'Can I help you?' she asked, in a slightly clipped but friendly way.

I told her that I had come to visit Chuck and that I understood that this was where he was to be found.

'Oh, yes,' she said chirpily, 'you can go in. He may not recognise you, but his parents are with him, so perhaps you would like to speak to *them*.'

For some reason, I had imagined that Chuck would be alone – which was rather stupid of me, I now realise – and I half wanted to turn away. But the nurse was standing there with such a welcoming expression upon her face that it would have been impossible for me to leave; so I simply gave myself to the action, and, after having knocked lightly upon the door, opened it and went in.

Chuck was in a bed opposite the entrance and his parents were sitting in chairs close to the door. 'Oh, hello,' I said, rather regretting the fact that Chuck's eyes were closed, 'I'm Richard. Chuck's flatmate.'

'Oh my!' cried his mother, as she rose to greet me. 'We've heard such a lot about *you*, Richard – haven't we, Ivan?'

'My goodness me, yes,' added Chuck's father, as he also rose to put out his hand. 'It's nice to meet you, Richard; and of you to come as well, I must say.'

I would have expected – wouldn't you? – that Chuck's parents would be enormous, but they were almost the opposite of that. Not midgets exactly, but certainly quite small; and I couldn't decide for the life of me which of them must be the blood-relative of Aunt Dodo.

Neither of them looked like Chuck. In fact, if anything, they seemed to resemble only each other; and I can remember thinking to myself that they possibly weren't Chuck's parents at all; and that, as is the case with the cuckoo and the nest, Chuck had been deposited with them falsely.

'Who is it?' I heard Chuck suddenly ask, without opening his eyes; and in a voice that seemed to have spoken out of the grave.

'Bruce, it's Richard,' said his mother, using Chuck's proper name and the one that his aunt had used at Bognor.

'Richard?' asked Chuck, as if the name was unfamiliar to him.

'Yes, *Richard*,' his mother replied. 'You know: who shares the flat with you.'

'Oh, Richard,' said Chuck with a kind of grin, but still

not opening his eyes, 'I thought he was in the country.'

'I was, Chuck,' I said, taking a step towards his bed. 'I've just got back. Darby got George to ring me from the hostel, and I left straight after lunch.'

Chuck remained silent, seeming unable to take this in.

'He's been in a coma, Richard,' his father explained, 'and is only just beginning to be out of it. But he'll be glad you are here, I am sure. He's talked such an awful lot about you.'

I felt rather embarrassed by this, and didn't quite know what to answer in reply – so I quickly asked them about the accident; about how serious it had been and so forth; and for a while we talked about that. And as we were doing so, I couldn't help staring at them from time to time, to see if I could find any reflection in them of Chuck. There really did seem to be none, however. And I remember thinking to myself that if the person who had claimed that he was my father should happen to be my real one, whatever proof he had of that identity, wouldn't necessarily lie in his physique.

'Will you be staying for a while?' Chuck's mother asked in a rather timid way. 'We've been here for hours, and – if we can, would like to go out for a meal. We've been offered tea and biscuits, but nothing else; and are shy of asking for something more substantial.'

'Please, don't worry,' I said, 'I'll be here. I can stay for as long as you like.'

'Oh, it won't be for long,' said Chuck's father, with a neat smile. 'We'll be gone for less than an hour, I should think. And then, Richard, perhaps you will allow me to drive you home.'

I wasn't too sure whether I was meant to accept this offer or not; but I thanked him for it and off they went – both of them smiling at me in exactly the same way, I thought: smiles that I am sure suppressed a deep anxiety, but that on the surface appeared quite cheerful.

For a while Chuck was silent; and being a tidy sort, I busied myself with his room – partly to have something to do, and also because I was a little compulsive about such matters. Then, as I was standing at the window of the room, looking down at the great swirl of traffic below, Chuck suddenly began questioning me about George; wanting to know how he had found my number in the country; whether or not he had met me at the station; and if he had, why it was that he hadn't come with me to the hospital.

I explained things briefly to him; saying that George had been busy; that he had made a previous arrangement and so forth; and that he would probably be coming to visit him the following day; but I wasn't too sure that he took it in. However, it was soon made clear to me that he had by no means lost his grip upon life, because all at once he sat upright in his bed, let out one of his enormous, animal-like roars, and asked me to find a bedpan.

'A *what*?' I asked, not being quite certain what he had said.

'A fucking *bed*pan!' he repeated. 'I've got to have a piss!'

'My God,' he said, once I had found it, and once he had placed it beneath the sheets, 'that's a relief. I've been dying to do that all afternoon.'

'Well, why *didn't* you?' I asked, a little annoyed with him.

'Why?' he said, now opening his eyes at last and looking at me in a sly sort of way that seemed to have some humour in it. 'Because I don't want the nurses to see my cock – that's why.'

'Oh, Chuck,' I said. 'Don't be stupid.'

'I'm not being stupid, Bo,' he said, now quite his old self again. 'That's all they think of – the whole bloody tribe of them.'

I had to laugh when he said this – and for a moment things

almost seemed normal; but he then let out another enormous roar, dropped his head back on to his pillow, turned swiftly on to his side, and immediately fell asleep.

Chuck didn't speak to me again that day; and when his parents returned, his father insisted upon driving me back to South Kensington. I protested a little against it, by saying that I could easily take a bus; but I had the impression that he'd be glad to have the diversion; and after I had wished Chuck's mother goodbye, I picked up my suitcase and off we went.

The car was a rather expensive one, I noticed; and it struck me that Chuck's parents were probably quite well off, which was something I'd given no thought to until then.

'Now,' said Chuck's father, as we purred our way towards Knightsbridge, 'just give me directions, Richard. I don't know this part as well as I should, I'm afraid. Do we go left – past Harrods – or do we take the upper road by the park?'

As we bore left down the Brompton Road, he asked if I had met his sister; and for a moment I couldn't think who it was that he was speaking about. 'I thought you'd been down to Bognor,' he said, when I didn't answer, 'or did Bruce make that up?'

Not much more was said between us; but I still couldn't help turning to stare at him occasionally as he sat beside me in the car; because it seemed so incredible that such a small, orderly figure should be both the father of Chuck and the brother of Chuck's Aunt Dodo. And as soon as we arrived at our destination, I thanked him and said goodbye, adding that I'd certainly be seeing Chuck the following day and hoped that we then might meet again.

It was a very odd feeling I had, as I undid the door of the flat; knowing that Chuck wouldn't be there. I still half expected to hear him making clattering noises in the kitchen; or to have him call out to me from his room. And it seemed even stranger when I imagined that I'd be there without him for some time.

Quite frankly, I don't really know whether I felt pleased about this or not. The one thing I was truly glad of was the idea that, during the time Chuck was to be away, George could both ring me and visit me freely; and I can recall how thinking that thought made my settling into the flat much easier. George was going to telephone me the following day; and with it being a Sunday, would probably go with me to the hospital. Even if he didn't want to see Chuck, I imagined that he would none the less accompany me.

However, as you know, nothing like that occurred; because, to repeat what I said a few pages ago, I heard nothing at all from George; neither on the Sunday, nor on the day after. And – in that I neither saw him nor spoke to him again, that parting between us on the Saturday, on the steps of St George's Hospital, proved to be our final, brief exchange.

In the last chapter I spoke of the astonishment I felt in relation to this; but what I have to explain to you is that my reason for using that word wasn't so much because George had failed to get in touch with me, and because he had disappeared so suddenly from my life; it was more because I had attempted to do nothing at all about it, and had made no effort to contact him.

After all, I knew perfectly well where he was; and that he was still living at the hostel; since he had rung me from there on the Saturday. And since I had even jotted down his number, and had then slipped it carefully into my wallet, I could easily have used it in order to speak to him – to ask if he was ill or something; or if there was some particular reason for his silence. Yet I had failed to do that; and that is what caused me my astonishment.

Had I known all along that this would happen? Could it be, perhaps – as I have half suggested to you before – that not only had George been using me, but that I had been using him; and that we each held for the other only a temporary meaning as a result? I really do believe that this was the case; and I think as well that, when we are young, a great number of people pass in and out of our lives in this way. Projections are formed speedily – and they are often intense ones – but it seems to me that they are able to dissolve themselves, and then fade, in an equally rapid fashion.

I often wonder what became of George; and why it was that he had taken the sudden decision not to be seeing me again. Did he go back to his girl, I sometimes wonder, or find someone new? Did he stay on at the hostel for a while, and then move into a flat – or had he not even stayed in London at all, and gone back to the banks of the Clyde?

I have no answers to this; and if our parting had been at a different moment – where there hadn't been Chuck's accident to cope with, for example – I daresay that I would have reacted to it more strongly, and been more disturbed by it than I was.

But to be honest with you, I am not even certain about that. When something truthful comes to the surface – by which I mean something you have really known about all along, but have prevented from forming itself into full consciousness – there is a kind of sweetness of feeling about it that is comforting: and I certainly recall having that type of feeling just then.

Strange though they were for me, those days that I spent alone in the flat in South Kensington, immediately after my return to London from the country, had a kind of serenity about them that was quite new to me; giving me the impression that the abrupt departure of George meant that I had not so much lost something on the outside as gained its equivalent in myself. Whether or not this could be said to be the 'George' in me I am not sure; but it certainly seems to have been something along those lines, because I know that I had a much steadier view of life than before; and one that was very similar in my mind to the one that I had always projected on to George.

I can see now, of course, that it was a much too gilded picture that I had made of him; but, nonetheless, it was one in which I believed; and I shall always be grateful to him on account of it. 'Friends come and go' is a Chinese saying that always appeals to me – and they do. The only constant in life is change; and it would be unwise I think to believe otherwise. For who would have imagined (and in this I include you, the reader, as well as myself) that within just a few days over a fortnight after my return to London from Reading, not only would George and I have parted, never to see each other again, but also the life that I shared with Chuck would have adopted such rough, such unruly proportions, that it would have forced itself to an end.

But life, as they say, can be a great deal stranger than fiction; and the tale that I have to tell must now move forward again. Which is why I must return to that odd break I made in my narrative, when, as opposed to my arrival at Paddington station, I chose to speak about Chuck's return from hospital; and how, after that distressing scene in the flat, when I had found the torn letter on the floor and a knife plunged into my pillow, I had managed to pack Chuck off to his parents and had made up my mind to leave.

The first thing I did was to ring Molly. You will recall, I expect, how earlier in the day, when we had been having coffee together in the kitchen, she had kindly given me her number; and I thought that the least I could do was to tell her of my decision, and to say that I was hoping to leave that night. Also, I wanted to ask if she would act as an intermediary – between Chuck and myself, I mean; because I didn't feel like writing him a letter, yet wanted to assure him that I would be leaving my keys in the flat – probably above the kitchen sink, I thought – and that, as far as the rent was concerned, I'd do what I could to send him at least my share of it for the next week or two; because I wasn't too sure that he could afford the place on his own.

When I told Molly this she laughed. 'Can't afford it!' she more or less shouted down the phone. 'Like my mother, his parents are rolling in money – or rather, his father is . . . Don't worry, Richard. I'll have a word with them' (meaning just his parents, I presumed, and not his Aunt Dodo). 'In any case, you've done right – in deciding to leave, I mean. Chuck needs to be on his own; and he always will . . . I know,' she added, 'because that's how I am myself.'

I thought it so honest of her, that I couldn't but admire her when she said that – and I then risked asking her why it was that if her family was so well off, Chuck was always ribbing her about money – about her wanting to beg or borrow it from people. And to my surprise, she said that it was just a joke – that was meant, she thought, to keep her in her place. 'He's always done it,' she had said, with a deep chuckle in her voice. 'I don't know why. Some daft quirk of his, I suppose.'

I chuckled with her in return about this; and then, because she was being so open and cheerful in general, I asked her what had happened that morning, when I had left her drinking with Chuck in the kitchen.

'Oh, he just went wild,' she replied, 'raving on about someone called George; saying he was doing you in, I think, or something mad like that. Then, when he started playing about with a knife, I got panicky and left. He'd drunk too much, Richard – too quickly. The liquor just went to his head.' He hadn't attacked her, you will be pleased to know; and her hand had been wrapped in a handkerchief only because she had grazed herself rather badly when she got up to get away.

'And where are you going to *go*?' Molly then asked, referring to my intention to leave that night. 'It's already gone five,' she said, 'so you'll have to stay on until tomorrow, at least. Be sensible, Richard. Now that Chuck's left, you don't *have* to act compulsively – do you? I mean, I can understand how you were feeling earlier; but surely now that he's gone, you can take your time – can't you? I mean, where for God's sake can you *go*, Richard, at this time of day?'

Looking back at it, I can see that what she was telling me was more than reasonable; and that, unlike the mother in Chuck, that side of her nature was positive. And I daresay you will be thinking to yourself that it was advice I ought to have followed. But my mind was too made up about the move; and on top of that, I was still full of the energy I had mustered, in order to cope with the madness of Chuck's behaviour; and knew no means of going against it.

'Oh, I'll find something,' I had said to Molly. 'If need be, I can go to the hostel, for instance, where Chuck and I met. Or if not that, I've seen some advertisements in a local tobacconist's window – often for rooms to let in the area – so I could try one of those. Tell Chuck,' I said, 'that I just *had* to go. And tell him too – will you? – that it isn't only because of him. Tell him there's another reason – a different one – that I can't explain; or that I can't speak about easily, at least. It's got nothing to do with George. Please make sure you tell him that. It has to do with my family.'

As soon as I used those words, they created a kind of echo within my brain, because they were words I'd not used before in my life. 'My family', I had said, almost as if I already had one; and which wasn't the case, of course: but I suspect that I had employed that term because it was what I was beginning to think of as my family that was now so occupying my mind. For what I've not told you is that by the time Chuck came home from the hospital, I had already called the solicitor's office, whose address was in Lincoln's Inn; and, after explaining the reason why I was ringing, had been given an appointment to meet the solicitor in what was now just two days' time.

And what I was so certain of was the strong need I felt to be on my own by then: to be settled somewhere – anywhere, so that I could cope properly with that event. In fact, so intense was the feeling I had concerning this, and concerning a possible meeting with my father, that I had already half pictured it in my dreams. The image had been unclear; and, as is so often the case with the unconscious, the figure it bred for itself was a somewhat ghostly one; and totally lacking in physicality. None the less, during the time that Chuck was away at the hospital, I recall how I woke several times from my sleep, thinking that someone (or perhaps something) was standing by my bed: which probably meant, I now realise, that my mind had been busy preparing itself, and making adjustments towards that encounter.

As soon as I had finished my telephone call to Molly, I put on my donkey-jacket and went out: telling myself that I must persist with my intention of leaving the flat that night, and that I shouldn't be swayed by Molly's suggestion that I'd do best to stay on there for a day or two. And a little to my surprise, I found what I wanted immediately. Rents weren't very high in those days, and just to the south of where we lived, it was easy to find a bed-sitting-room, for example; often in the basements of the huge, stuccoed Victorian houses that surrounded the garden squares. It wouldn't be heated, of course, and its furniture would be drab; but it would probably be spacious rather than cramped, and not without its own muted kind of grace.

Such then was the room that I found that evening. The woman who answered the phone had a rather posh, suspicious-sounding voice, and was immediately aggressive about the fact that I was ringing her after six; but once I had explained (which wasn't at all true) that I wasn't allowed to telephone from the office; and that I was in need of a room immediately and could offer her a fortnight's rent in advance, she quickly changed her attitude; and said that, providing I could be there before eight o'clock, the bed-sitting-room would be mine.

In certain ways it wasn't a pleasant feeling, to have to pack my things in such a hurry. Fortunately, I had very few books to take, or heavy articles of that kind. There should have been *The Mystery of the Virgin*, of course, but I have an idea that I must have left it behind in a cupboard, because I certainly don't recall having it with me after the move. And I had no domestic objects – no pots, pans, pictures – not even a clock, as I remember. So it wasn't such an enormous task to gather my things together, and to be able to move out quickly.

All the same, I did feel sad in a way, when I went to switch the light off in my room; and when I paused there for a while, on seeing those dreamlike towers beyond its window that belonged to those temples of Art and of Science. The life I had shared with Chuck hadn't been all roses, as you well know; but it had been rich and various, and full of the most unexpected perspectives; so that if I had been 'green', as Chuck had described me, when he spoke on the phone to Jack at Bognor, to see if we could visit his aunt for the weekend, it seems to me that, whilst I was still far from being mature, I was certainly a lot less 'verdant', as I might put it, than when I had first met Chuck at the hostel; and before we had moved into the flat.

Had Chuck simply been jealous of George? And had his savage stabbing of my pillow, combined with the tearing up of my letter – the letter from George, that is – been just a crude expression of that? I really don't think so. I may have painted Chuck with too broad a brushstroke at times, and made him seem too primitive as a result; but fierce and bold though they were, I think that Chuck's general character and make-up were much less simple than one might imagine.

What so angered him, it seems to me; and what drove him towards his particular brand of madness; was not that he was too primitive or naive, or too embedded in his self-ignorance. It was more the opposite of that, in that he had seen and known too much.

Unlike myself, he had been forced to face himself when he was young; and although he may have been angered by what he had seen, he had, none the less, accepted his personal tragedy in a direct and honest fashion. And it was because of *this*, I think, not jealousy, that he had sought to warn me about George; because he had seen so clearly, as he once put it, 'what that bastard is up to.'

People's motives, it would appear, are seldom as crude or as simple as they give the effect of being on the surface; and certainly as far as my own motives were concerned, I can see that behind all my actions at that time there lay a myriad of intentions; and you could easily say to me that the 'use' I had made of George – or, for that matter, the 'use' I had made of Chuck – could in itself be described as questionable.

However, to go more deeply into that kind of thing would require another kind of book; so allow me please to take up my story-line again – and to do so on the morning just two days later, when I was due to keep my appointment with the solicitor; which was after I had moved out of the flat and was installed in my new abode – which, as I said, did turn out to be one of those drab, spacious bed-sitting-rooms, I described a couple of pages ago; but which – perhaps because it was so featureless in general – seemed to provide the breathing space that I had been needing, before my life moved forward again.

## XII

HAVE YOU EVER been to Lincoln's Inn? It is an impressive place – or the part of it was that *I* visited, at least. An enclosed square – or green, rather, surrounded by a fine set of late-seventeenth-century buildings, each with a small flight of steps placed before its entrance, and not at all used for what you might think – for domestic purposes, that is – but given over entirely to the law – or, rather, to people in the service of the law – by which I mean barristers, solicitors and the like: so that the whole place is a kind of web of rooms and passageways, many filled with files and papers and with telephones constantly ringing; and with people making money out of other people's worries and concerns, which seems to be the main occupation of that somewhat parasitic profession.

Knowing a little of this, I feared that I might all too easily be overcome by the general atmosphere of the place; and with that in mind, decided that I would first take a bus to Piccadilly, and then go on from there by taxi; thinking to myself that this would be the cheapest way of my arriving in some style; and thinking too, that if the taxi-driver knew the address – which was highly probable, I thought – it would avoid my having to look for it.

However, my little plan didn't prove to be as wise a move as I had hoped; because it meant that in no time, I had been deposited at the entrance to the solicitor's; and before I had chance to adjust myself, was being ushered by a quietly spoken secretary into Mr Sweeting's office: Mr Sweeting being a partner of 'Howard, Starkey & Sweeting', which was the name of the firm in full; and the office, as I have called it, being more the opposite of that; since it was a well-proportioned room that contained a number of fine pieces of furniture; and that, with it being placed on the first floor of the building, and being one that overlooked the square, gave the impression of belonging to some gracious gentlemen's club.

'Oh, yes!' exclaimed this long-legged, reedy-looking figure, as he rose to shake my hand, and as I advanced towards where he was standing behind a generous antique desk; upon which, I observed, was spread a stretch of heavy green baize cloth, bearing some silver-topped ink bottles and the like. 'Now – let me see. It's Mr Constable – isn't it?'

I quickly assured him that this was so; and then, as he began to fiddle with a sheaf of typewritten papers, that he had quickly placed in front of him, he asked if we had already spoken to one another on the telephone; to which he then added, without giving me an opportunity to reply, 'No. I don't think we have – have we? So you must know little or nothing about this matter.'

I explained to him how I had been contacted by Mr Carson (saying first, of course, who Mr Carson was) and how it had been through him that I had come to read the letter – meaning, of course, the one that he, Mr Sweeting, had written to the police station in Berkshire. And much to my surprise (just because I hadn't been warned of it, I suppose) he said that Mr Carson had been in touch with him.

'I knew I'd spoken to someone,' he said with a wan smile. 'Carson – yes. He rang just a few days ago; saying that I should be expecting you to contact me – and which, of course, you now have.'

I simply smiled when he said this; mostly because I was nervous and didn't know what to say. And then (after he had allowed his eyes to take me in more carefully, I thought; and had made me wonder whether I was dressed in a decent enough fashion) he said, 'Now, Mr Constable; I think I must first tell you that my client, as I must speak of him – whose name is Sir Edmund Pallister, by the way – is extremely anxious to meet you; and with that in mind, I have made arrangements for him to be here in a little less than an hour from now: unless of course,' he went on, 'you have some objection to such a meeting; in which case, I would need to have my secretary call him immediately . . . And please believe me,' he continued yet again, 'I don't think there is much doubt about the identity of my client – in relation to yourself, I mean . . . I can't think, to be quite frank with you, that I have ever handled a case such as this before, if one can call it that. Most of my business – or a great deal of it, at least – concerns the exchanges of property and so forth – inheritance and the like – and it is quite a novelty for me to be handling what by comparison is a rather delicate matter. So if I should seem clumsy at all, or a little over-direct, you must excuse me.'

In spite of the fact that I was really thinking the opposite (in that he had blurted out so much at me so quickly, and that I hadn't had time to take it in) I told him that I didn't think he was being clumsy; and that in any case, as far as my being without parents was concerned, I was used to being thought different.

'Oh, yes – I can understand that,' he said. 'We all take our having parents too much for granted, I am afraid. Until now, in fact, I don't think I have pictured to myself what it must be like to be without them.'

'Most people haven't,' I replied a little curtly, causing him to pause for a second, and to peer at me over his spectacles.

'No,' he said, in a rather detached kind of way, 'I don't suppose they have . . . Anyway,' he went on, 'you aren't to be without a father for much longer. Before we speak more about this matter, I would like to make that clear to you, Mr Constable. And it is why Sir Edmund is anxious to meet you today – rather than wait . . . Now, I realise that this is a lot for you to take in. Have you heard of Sir Edmund, do you think? You might have done, since his name is occasionally in the papers. He is quite a figure, here in the City.'

I told him that I did think I had heard the name, in spite of it being untrue; because I felt that if I had chosen to say the opposite, he might possibly have been offended. But he took little notice of my words, and again began fumbling among the papers on his desk.

'I think,' he then said, taking up a large envelope; and without bothering, I thought, about what my own feelings might be; 'that the best thing I can do is to ask you to read this letter. I won't say who it is from. I'd rather not have to, to tell you the truth; but as you will see, it is addressed to your father – to Sir Edmund, that is, and has been sent care of myself. Sir Edmund and I have been friends for years: for years and years, in fact; and we have both agreed that rather than have me explain the letter's contents – which I'd not care to do, in any case – it would be best if you were allowed to read it quietly, to yourself. It is a very personal letter – and a distressing one too, I must warn you of that; but it will explain everything to you. So I think that to read it is what you should do first . . . Now,' he said, rising a second time

189

from his desk, 'if you will come with me – over here; and into this other room; I'll leave the letter with you; so that you can read it without interruption.

'There,' he said, as he led me into a room that was placed next to his own, 'you won't be disturbed in here at all; I can promise you that. And once you have read the letter, it will be much easier for us to discuss matters in general. And as I said to you just now, Mr Constable, you will excuse me – won't you? – if I am being a trifle too blunt, or unfeelingful, perhaps. You do appreciate, I hope, that this sort of thing isn't exactly in my line, so to speak; although for your sake, I am so pleased, of course – and for Sir Edmund's too. It isn't often that one has the task of uniting a father with his son; and as I said to you before, this letter will supply the proof you need that that is what you are to each other . . . Now, I'll leave you to it, if I may. That is a comfortable chair – over there by the window; and if you would care for such a thing, I can have you sent in some tea; or perhaps some coffee; whichever you would prefer.'

I told him that I didn't think I needed either; partly because it was true; and also, if I'm to be honest, because I'd been made rather shy by this sudden attention; and because it seemed a shock to my general system to find myself treated in this way. And there was also a further reason, of course – which was that I had been so intrigued by what he had told me about my being the son of someone well known; and because I was feeling somewhat in awe of that. And I was also wondering who the letter might be from, and what exactly it might be about; and didn't want to be interrupted, as I was reading it, by someone bringing me coffee.

Once Mr Sweeting had closed the door of the room, I more or less dashed across to the window to look down at the square below. It was a really beautiful day, with the rays of the pale, mid-morning sun filtering through the still leafless branches of the trees, and casting a web of constantly shifting patterns upon the two painted shutters of the room, which guarded its elegant, low-set window. There was a strong wind blowing, and I noticed that people were hurrying to and fro as if the temperature was low; which caused me to think to myself that the entire morning had been like that; as if some strong wind had been blowing, and as if everything had been hurried. My arrival by taxi had seemed to be that; and so had the way in which I had been ushered so swiftly by the secretary into Mr Sweeting's office. And he too had seemed to be rushed, as if he was short of time.

Perhaps, I told myself, it was all because of this letter. Perhaps, I thought, nothing would make sense or begin to slow down until its contents had been read. So rather than be lingering there by the window, why, I wanted to know, hadn't I picked the letter up; and why hadn't I opened it; and hadn't I settled down to reading it?

I suppose the answer to that must be that it had all been simply too much; and that I was needing a pause to catch my breath; although what exactly my mind was doing just then I don't recall. What I do remember is that I began toying with the idea that providing my parents had been married, my real name must be Pallister; and if they hadn't, and if that meant I was illegitimate, would my name be changed, I wondered, by some particular legal process: one that might involve it being advertised in the newspapers and the like?

I must have continued having that type of fantasy for some time; because I can remember how I began considering the idea that I was lacking the will to read the letter; but some noise, I think – perhaps of a door being slammed – forced me to pull myself together; and so, without any further ado, I turned from where I had been standing and crossed to read the letter at a small desk; choosing this rather than the large, tapestried armchair that Mr Sweeting had suggested.

As you know, the letter was in a largish envelope; and it consisted of about five broad sheets of cream-coloured paper, some of which appeared to be stained by liquid of a kind – possibly by tea, I thought – and all of which were written in a large, rather scrawly-looking hand – perhaps, I told myself, by someone who was either old or ill; and in a hand that appeared to change and vary as it proceeded from page to page. There was no address to act as a heading, and no date; but the handwriting was large and clear, and I was able to read it easily. This is what the letter said –

Dear Edmund,

How am I to write this letter? I have strength enough to begin it, but whether or not to end it is another matter. There is so much for me to say, and I have so little time in which to say it. Another thing, is where I am going to send it, since I have no idea of your address, and can only think that you might still be in touch with Geoffrey Sweeting – so perhaps I shall send it care of him. And if it reaches you – and I must somehow convince myself that it will – please forgive me for its length and for the appalling hand in which it is written. The truth is that I am gravely ill and have been for some time, and the doctors have given me only a few more weeks in which to live. One part of me says to itself that they aren't always right, and that in a year from now I might still be lingering on, but another is more sure that what they are saying is true. When death is at your door, there seem to be signs that it is so, and during these past few days, they have shown themselves to me regularly.

How are you, Edmund? I've read about you in the newspapers from time to time, and you appear to be flourishing. But there has been no mention of whether you have married or not. I imagine that you have though, and that you are probably blessed with a fine, sturdy set of children who reflect the constancy of your nature. If you are, then I bless them with all my heart, and if they and your wife should happen to read what I say here, I must ask them not to think badly of me, or to see me as something that is dark or ugly.

I am bound to appear to them as being something of that kind. I am aware of that. My temperament, as you well know, was never a very stable one, and I often wonder why it is that I have been so wilful over things, and so incapable of checking myself. Was it something I inherited – a kind of madness that has been passed down to me? Or was it simply that my parents never checked me when I was young? I shall never know. All I do know is that, during the past year or two, I have often thought of what we were to each other. How deeply – how passionately we were in love, and how foolish I was to destroy it all, to behave so wildly and irrationally, accusing you of things that I knew were not true – causing you so much hurt and pain. And then, when we seemed almost on the point of becoming engaged, simply cutting myself off from you as I did, and so from all the goodness that you stood for.

Why? – I have voiced that word to myself a thousand times, even a million ones, perhaps. What awful anger, or what jealousy possessed me? The mind is such a peculiar thing. For some reason, my own has left me with no peace. Frail though I am, I am still restless. Some madness in me still fights with something or with someone. Over the years, I've learned to curb myself a little, but it's still in me. Even now, when I know that I must prepare myself for what is on the other side of the grave, I am still given to bouts of anger that even drugs are unable to control, and the only real peace I seem to have found has been through the steadfast love of my sister, Bridget – whose name, at least, you may remember – and also through the almost motherly care and kindness of the dear, generous-hearted person with whom I have lived for the past twelve years, who is partly an invalid herself, and for whom I have acted as a companion.

She is a wonderful character. A little deaf, I am afraid, but since she makes such fun of it at times, all the richer for it, it would seem. You would both love and admire her – I am quite sure of that. She is so stoical, and never dwells upon her infirmities – in being disabled, I mean. Her husband died some years ago, before I met her, but she has a daughter who visits her regularly, and a nephew too. And both of them have been kind to me.

However, if it were only to speak to you of all this, I would never be writing you this letter – knowing, as I do, that it is bound to come as an intrusion into whatever life you may have made for yourself, and that it could easily prove an embarrassment both to yourself and to your family. I may have been wilful and ill-tempered in the extreme. I may have been driven by the most horrible compulsions that have been beyond my power to control, but at least I have seen them as being part of my own limitations, and have done my best not to project them on to others.

I must have hurt you badly, Edmund, and in doing so, I no doubt damaged you in some way. But it was never meant as an act of evil. So you must believe me when I say that there is nothing of that kind behind this letter. Nothing of revenge, I mean, or things of that kind. Nor, for that matter, is there – or was there, rather – behind what is so painful for me to write about now, yet which I have to do, before it is too late.

I cannot do it this very night. My eyes are already weary, and it is only just past six o'clock. But perhaps tomorrow evening, I shall be able to take up my pen again. I must pray to be given the strength to do that – otherwise there will have been no point in my writing at all. For it can hardly interest you to know the things I have said so far. You don't need to be told that I have been wilful and destructive – you know that only too well. And I don't deserve any interest on your part, concerning the way in which I have passed my time during the years since we were together. Before I begin again, however – and just in case you should read what I am writing eventually – let me ask you now that if you are unable to forgive me for what I have done, you will excuse me, at least. To know that – or to be able to think it, rather – will count a lot for me . . .'

Here the letter broke off, and there were more stains on the paper. Whether or not they had been caused by tears, as I half imagined, I don't know; but the rest of that page was blank; and it was only on the following sheet (which I noticed was a great deal more creased and crumpled than the others) that the writing began again.

Another day, and I'm still here; still able to hear the sea. Still able to look at it from my window. When I woke up this morning it seemed a miracle. I had so tired myself yesterday, not just by the physical effort of writing, but also by the emotion it had stirred up in me, so that my sleep has been torn and broken by the strain of it all, and I have tossed and turned all night.

But that is no matter. What I am so glad of, and why I spoke of it being a miracle, is that I am feeling such a lot stronger today – and certainly strong enough, I think, for me to be able to say to you what I now must – horribly painful though it will be.

Oh, Edmund! – how shall I tell you, when I can hardly tell myself, that you have a son – our son – and that I have kept his existence not only a secret from yourself but from everyone! From my family, my sister, and my friends. For a full quarter of a century – yes, it's been as long as that – I've held it bottled up inside me.

I'll spare you the details of how I cut myself off from people – from the whole world, as you might say – once I knew that I was pregnant. It is astonishing what clever means the will can invent. What savagery in me made me do it, I really can't say. But I did do it, and I am responsible for it, whether I like the idea that I am or not. But what I do so want you to know is that the child was perfectly healthy, and that, during the first few weeks of his life, when I had him with me, I lavished upon him all the loving care and devotion of any decent, normal mother. Then, however, I did what I have regretted ever since – by which I mean that I abandoned him, setting him down upon the steps of a police station in Berkshire, in a basket.

That sounds like something out of a storybook – doesn't it? Why in Berkshire? you might well ask. Well, that is partly because it is where I had gone in order to hide myself from the world, and also because it is where I grew up when I was small, before my parents moved to London. Perhaps too, the very smallness of the place made me want to use it as I did. However, I wasn't entirely without thought or concern, since I lingered there for long enough to be sure the baby had been found – as, indeed, I had imagined he might be, by one of the constables of the station, as he returned to take up his duties. A burly man, as I remember, who gathered the child's basket into his arms and rocked it to and fro. He must have been a good man – a true father. And when I think of it now, it pains me to have to remember how I have robbed you of all that. Of all the joy there must be in watching a child grow up – in seeing him first walk and talk. In knowing him as well as you know yourself.

I have robbed myself in that respect as well, of course, but as I say, that is a responsibility I have carried for a very long time indeed. What has been, and still is more difficult, is to carry the one I bear towards you.

Can you forgive me? Or as I said before, can you excuse me at least? – and put it down to something that is irrational, and that belongs to the darker side of nature? I cannot tell what it is that has made me guard my secret all these years, any more than I can tell why I have now chosen to release it, for there is some wild part of me that is still reluctant to give it up.

On a separate sheet of paper, I shall give you the address of my sister, here in Sussex – at Bognor, and also the address of the police station in Berkshire where I left the child. To which I shall add the date, time etc. I often wonder what became of him. Whether he grew up to become the fine, healthy boy he showed signs of doing, when I first held him in my arms. With these details, there is a chance at least of your tracing him, and of your being able to get in touch with him.

I cannot write more to you today, except to make out that extra sheet, giving you the various details I described. Whether or not I am to be given the extra strength I shall need to add a few further things tomorrow, remains, alas, to be seen. But at least I have managed to impart to you the important ones.

Goodnight Edmund – and if I can, I will write a little more to you in the morning. If not, I send you my love – if that is a thing worth having from me at all. About a year ago, I saw in the newspapers that you have been made a knight of the realm, and that impressed me a lot. And knights in shining armour do shining deeds – don't they? So will you make my amends for me, do you think, for all the horrible wilfulness that is inside me, and that has plagued me all these years? I may not deserve that, but our son does. It must be a dreadful thing, not to know who brought you into this world. That at least you can put right – although whether you will be able to repair the damage I have caused is another thing again.

Think kindly of me if you can. And think too that for some people, life's not an easy passage, and the seas on which they travel are turbulent ones, for which they cannot really be held responsible. I know that that has been the case with me. Nothing else will explain to me my actions. Certainly not my character, for instance, in which, in common with the majority of people, I am capable of being as good and as kind as anyone.

Goodnight again – and until the postscript that I plan to add tomorrow.

Yours ever, and most truthfully,
Florence

There was no postscript, and what I was able to read into its absence troubled me considerably, causing my hand to tremble more than a little, as I refolded the letter with care, and as I then replaced it in its envelope.

And as for the extra page, giving the various details that

had been mentioned, that had obviously been removed. Not that I had much difficulty in guessing its contents, of course; nor can it be necessary, I think, to add that my mind just then was in a highly keyed-up state, with so many complex thoughts and feelings, all whirling about inside me.

However, I told myself that I must somehow manage to keep calm – or to keep my balance, at least. From how it had appeared to me just a few hours ago, the view I had of myself had changed; and had done so so rapidly, and so dramatically, that I was feeling both dazzled and confused: so much so, in fact, that when I looked up from reading the letter, I wasn't quite certain of where I was; and it required some time for me to adapt to the idea that I was in a room in Lincoln's Inn; and in one that was adjacent to a solicitor's, whose name I had temporarily forgotten.

It would be flattering for me to know that you have been as involved by all this as I was at the time. But I suspect, somehow, that that is wishful thinking on my part; and that for various reasons – some to do with the devices I have employed – you will have retained throughout this story a degree of mental detachment. And certainly enough, I am inclined to imagine, not only to have worked out in your mind exactly who my mother was, but also – through that brief tale about Jack and Bridget – how her death had already been made known to me – inadvertently, through Molly.

For me, however, there had not been enough time as yet to do that; and it was only much later in the day that the different fragments of my story began to assemble themselves in my head; and that I was able to make full sense of the letter's contents; and so piece its jagged jigsaw together. For what you have to remember is that, although I had been half stunned by all that I had read, I was none the less still partly conscious of the fact that I might soon be meeting my father; and that however deeply moved I had been by all the various things that I had just learned, the psychic space that was then surrounding me was a great deal more cramped than I would have liked; so that, however upset I may have been made by all that had been thrust so suddenly into my mind, I still felt a need, somewhere inside me, to hold myself in readiness for that encounter.

No sooner had I placed the letter on top of the desk in front of me, than I heard voices in the next room; and on account of them I stood up; thinking, perhaps, that someone was about to enter. Then I heard Mr Sweeting say, 'Yes, Edmund, Richard is here. If you will just be patient for a moment, I'll check to see that he is ready.'

Unfortunately, I cannot relate to you what my reactions were to these words; all I can tell you is that they were followed by a brief pause, before I heard a steady knock on the door; and before it was then pushed open by Mr Sweeting.

'Finished?' he asked, with a nervous grin on his face, which caused his eyebrows to rise swiftly over his spectacles in what I thought was a comical fashion. And then, when I just nodded to him in reply, I recall how he glanced swiftly at the letter, as if he didn't feel certain that I had read it.

'Richard, your father is here,' he said, in a near whisper – and then I saw entering behind him a striking, middle-aged figure who so exactly resembled myself, that the image startled me.

He was a little taller than I was, perhaps, and he didn't have the same awkward, pigeon-boned chest that thrust itself out at the front; but his features were almost identical to my own, and apart from a few greyish streaks at the temples, he had the same wispy, bluish-black hair, the forelock of which had been combed neatly away from his forehead.